P9-APW-318

GRACE EDWARDS

The Blind Alley

iUniverse, Inc.
New York Bloomington

iUniverse books may be ordered through booksellers or by contacting:

iUniverse
1663 Liberty Drive
Bloomington, IN 47403
www.iuniverse.com
1-800-Authors (1-800-288-4677)

ISBN: 978-1-4502-5299-7 (sc)
ISBN: 978-1-4502-5300-0 (ebook)

Printed in the United States of America

iUniverse rev. date: 1/20/2011

SYNOPSIS:

Harlem 1954

Released after serving two years of a ten year sentence for murder, 24 year old Richard (Rhino) Lee Brown returns to Harlem to live with his grandmother.

His return has a profound effect on the 7 families in the small tenement and on the habitués of the 'Blind Alley', the after hours spot in the basement.

The Tenants

Apt #1 – (Lobby floor) Jimmie 'Blue' Williams , age 36, owner and operator of the 'Blind Alley', an afterhours jazz spot in the basement of 1048.

Apt #2A – Matthew Paige, musician, his wife Sandra, and son Theo, age 15.

Apt #2B – Fannie Dillard, grandmother of Richard (Rhino) Lee Brown.

Apt#3A – Effie Cummings. widow, age 35

Apt 3B – Clothilde & Stanislaw Morgan and daughter, Sara, age 15

Apt 4A – Rose Jordan, Cyrus Greene's niece, age 24

Apt 4B – Cyrus Greene, Rose's uncle, age 42

Prologue

The mist had nearly emptied the streets when Rhino stepped off the 8th Avenue bus and he was alone on the corner of 148th Street. He narrowed his eyes behind his thick lenses and strained to see how long it took before the outline of the vehicle dissolved, not so much into the hot August darkness as into the well of his own defective vision.

The bus lumbered uptown and out of sight yet he lingered, caught now by the on-off neon flash from the Peacock Bar and Grill across the street. He stared at the brightly bird above the entrance as the huge neon plume showered a brilliant array of light on the sidewalk. One of the feathers in the plume lit out of sequence, stayed brighter longer and seemed to turn off when it felt like it.

The bar appeared to be crowded, full of weekend noise. Two years ago, before everything had happened, he would not have noticed the lights and would have walked in without missing a beat. But that was before everything had happened. Now he could not move. He stared harder, expecting at any minute to hear the laughter, hear the grunts, and then feel the pain to the back of his head, the side of his face, and the hollow between his shoulders. Feel it again, again, and again until the laughter faded and the fingers of light turned crimson and spun away in the dark.

He glanced quickly over his shoulder. No one was there. Sound had come only from the wet squeal of a bus headed downtown. Its high beams pushed aside the wavery shadows as it passed, then it disappeared.

Finally he moved across the slick pavement, passed the corner grocery store with its streaked windows and made his way up three steps to number 1048, a small red brick nondescript tenement that seven families called home. He paused in the faded marble lobby and looked around disinterestedly. He was, finally, also home.

The steel framed door leading to the rear courtyard was ajar and the familiar sounds drifted toward him. Piano, horn, and scattered drum rolls, muted by the rain water trickling through the drain pipe. The notes seemed deliberate and disjointed, as if the musicians had given up practice and were experimenting in some private place. The pause between beats, however, was thick with laughter.

He sat on the steps, listening, with his small suitcase resting on his knees. "So, The Alley's still going strong. How about that. Ah, maybe... maybe she's there."

In one motion, he rose to his feet, unfolding his gaunt frame and pushing the shabby suitcase into the shallow recess under the stairs. "Damn bitch. Wasn't for her, none of this shit would've happened."

He moved from habit, like a cat, down the narrow wood steps and into the surrounding darkness toward the music, his colorless fingers fanning the ran-slick walls.

In the courtyard, the rain hung like a dark curtain, obscuring the passageway leading to The Alley but he did not pause.

"Pulled a damn long stretch. For what? For nuthin'. But I'm back. Even if I don't stay, I'm gonna let these son of a bitches know what they done. And somebody – Matthew, Cyrus, and especially that Rose-somebody's gonna pay."

Chapter One

APT 2A

August 1954

Matthew Paige, sax player and lead man of the 'Jazz Net' the tight combo that kept the Blind Ally jammed on the weekends, hadn't intended to fall asleep on the sofa but the heat had drawn everything out of him. The curtains hung limp in the window and what breeze there was, blew in hot and steamy. He had closed his eyes, intending to take five, and rise again refreshed enough to do something around the apartment.

Instead, he had fallen asleep and dreamed he was being stabbed in the throat. He saw the knife, gripped in a pale disembodied hand, descend in a tight arc. It severed his windpipe and vocal cords and splattered blood over the sofa where he lay. He wanted to scream out for his wife, but sound was frozen somewhere in his chest. He was going to die.

"Matt!" Sandra leaned over the sofa, shaking him. "Matt. Wake up. What in the world is on your mind to make you grunt and groan like that?"

He woke, bathed in the sweat of fright and August heat. The television was on, just as he had left it, stilled tuned to the McCarthy hearings. Sandra clicked the set off. "Why were you looking at television anyway, with your head hurting the way it is?"

Matthew rubbed his eyes, trying to remember. The room was so hot he could barely breathe. Earlier he had taken off his shirt and pants.

Now he looked at his arms and legs, red brown, tight muscled, and damp with sweat. He brushed his hands to his forehead.

"I don't know. I –"

Sandra handed him a headache powder and a glass of lemonade. "McCarthy." She was careful to speak softly. "Who needs to watch all that noise on television? That communisim stuff is none of black folks business."

Matthew frowned. "Try telling that to Paul Robeson when he was ambushed at that Peekskill rally...Even the cops joined in."

He could have gone on but it was too hot to argue. How long had he slept. Better to drain the glass before the ice melted. The tart sweet taste nearly loosened the constriction in his temples but he knew that his pain, part heat but mostly champagne hangover, would take time before subsiding.

And the nightmare didn't help.

He concentrated on the beat in his head, brought on by the all-night party for Big Buster, the number banker, that had had the Blind Alley Social Club in the basement jammed, the drinks flowing like a broken water main, and the noise of Blue's cash register humming above everything.

Matthew dimly remembered the closing number. The Jazz Net sound, cool and loose, had kept the crowd on its feet and the walls vibrating until 7 a.m. Now, after too little sleep, his head felt hollow and someone was tapping a large brick against it.

He vaguely remembered turning off the window fan in order to hear the television but found that the whir of the fan held more substance than the drone of the pinch-faced politicians on the screen.

Then he must have fallen asleep. And dreamt the dream which he could not now remember.

"I must be getting old, Sandy. How come I can't even remember a dream, a bad dream. I hope it didn't have any good digits. We could use some extra change."

Sandra eased onto the sofa beside him, her small frame nearly enveloped in the silk print pillows. Her light brown hair was brushed back from her face and held together at the nape of her neck by a wide green ribbon. When she spoke, her voice was soft but her words were clear. "Forget the numbers, Matthew. How are you gonna play again tonight? You're in terrible shape."

Mathew placed the glass on the table and looked at her. "Sandy, I haven't missed a weekend since the Alley opened and I don't intend to miss tonight. Blue hired me to entertain and that's what I'm gonna do. Maybe I'll sit back and let Maxie or Cee take the lead but I'll definitely be there."

He was looking at the saxophone stand near the piano as if it were another person in the room.

Sandra followed his gaze and decided that death was the only thing that would stop him and even after, his spirit would probably ease back and sit in just to keep the boys on key.

"Have it your way," she sighed "but this burning the candle at both ends has got to stop sometime. You're thirty seven years old. You have a day job, and you have a wife and son to think about."

She picked up the empty pitcher and left him to wrestle with his hangover. The room was mercifully quiet and Matthew lay on his back, this time intending to study the cracks in the ceiling.

*** ***

When he woke again, the sunlight had faded to purple and a cooler breeze blew through the open window.

In the kitchen, he read the note propped against the covered dinner plate.

Theo needs new sneakers. We'll be back by 8.

Matthew crumpled the paper. "Damn. I promised to take the boy shopping. The whole day just slipped away."

He moved through the silence toward the bathroom, following the thread of dream he struggled to remember. But even the icy shower was not enough to recall the wraith-like image that floated just on the other side of memory.

...dream probably didn't mean a thing except to let me know that champagne is too rich for my blood. Need to stick to my scotch. Tasty, tried, and true.

He turned up the tiny radio on the bathroom hamper and caught the tail end of an Illinois Jacquet solo. How High The Moon. The notes were mellow and managed to dislodge some of the hard knots inside his head as he showered.

Later, though Sandra and Theo had not returned, he dressed, picked up his horn and headed downstairs. He knew that most of his guys were already downstairs rehearsing, getting a jump on the evening.

The mist was cool against his skin and the slight ache in his feet let him know that steady rain was coming. But he still needed to take his usual walk around the block, get some fresh air in his lungs before heading inside.

*** ***

The Blind Alley Social and Athletic Club, situated at the end of a dark corridor in the basement of Matthew's building, usually opened around nine, was crowded by midnight, and jammed to the walls at 3.a.m. when the regular bars closed.

As long as Matthew had been playing there, the only athletics he had witnessed occurred when Big Blue, the owner, had to bounce an occasional troublemaker. The 'athletic' part was dropped when Blue acquired his .38 Special and posted a sign that announced -

Welcome to the Blind Alley

Check All Hats, Coats, Artillery,

And Attitudes at the Door

OR ELSE!!

And since that time, had maintained order on his reputation alone.

Most folks were regulars who drifted in after the Peacock Bar across the avenue closed for the night. Matthew wondered what would happen if The Alley were ever raided. There was, as far as he knew, only one entrance and the thought made him nervous when he allowed himself to think about it, which was not too often.

He lingered on the corner, watching the strollers. The air was heavy and the small scatter of raindrops would soon develop into a steady pour, yet 8th Avenue was a parade of Saturday night movie, dance, and flashing party colors. Under their umbrellas, people were going places. Others were rushing home from hairdressers, cleaners, and barbershops to prepare to join them. The Alley would be jammed also, despite the rain.

He returned to the building, moved through the lobby, and paused at the rear door. As usual, there was no light leading down the stairs to the courtyard and, as usual, he counted the steps in the dark,

Midway through the corridor, a brush of movement behind him – too loud for a cat or the dry scratch of a rat – stopped him in his tracks.

...who's that??

He turned back toward the mouth of the corridor, moving fast, not wanting to be caught where he had no room to maneuver. And not wanting to think of Sandra's warnings:

'Matthew, you make good money at the Post Office. Nine to five. Five days a week. Why hang out in an after hours spot?'

And he: assuring her that the Blind Alley was safe (compared to some of the joints where folks had to cut their way in and shoot their way out but he never mentioned those clubs.)

Now here he was, easing along a dark corridor with neither a gun nor a knife, only his saxophone for which he would rather die than use to defend himself. He held the case under his arm and peered out, scanning the courtyard. The rain was hard now, drumming staccato atop the garbage cans.

" ...Nothing. Just this hangover still hanging on. Got me jumping at nothing."

He turned again and moved quickly toward the club.

*** ***

The place was large and the black painted low ceiling sparkled with aluminum stars. The essence of last night's cigarettes and whisky clotted the air but Jimmy was there, hunched over the keys, and Maxie strummed his bass, picking up Jimmy's rhythm. Philly, the drummer, leaned back taking a last drag on his smoke before picking up his sticks. The shimmer of small candles in tin saucers reflected the waxed surfaces of the tables circling the dance area and several patrons had already arrived.

Blue called from behind the bar, "man, everybody's here. What took you so long?" and Matthew smiled, ready for the night, ready to believe that the sound in the corridor had been a figment of his imagination, just like the dream that earlier wakened him in that cold sweat.

*** ***

Midnight.

From the small stage, Matthew peered out onto the crowd, waved to the dancers on the floor nearest him, then focused on the band again. Jimmy, still hunched over the piano, ended his solo and Maxie eased in. Matthew listened to descending chromatic bass line and raised his horn, waiting to pick up the cue. He was feeling good and the horn would deliver the feeling to the crowd.

But the split second between Maxie's note and his own was fractured by a noise that carried above the shading of the music and the low buzz of the patrons. Someone had fallen over or knocked over a chair. The dancers turned to look and stopped dancing. Small talk faded into flat silence.

Blue, pouring a drink at the bar, squinted toward the noise and put the bottle down. "Well ain't this some shit!"

On the bandstand, Matthew tried to look beyond the narrow glare of the spotlight but caught only a vague movement. The figure came into focus as it approached the bar.

"Well, I'll be damned." Matthew signaled the bassist to keep the beat, although the dancers appeared frozen. Then he stepped off the stage.

"Well, well. Didn't expect to see you back so soon, Rhino."

The man turned to scrutinize Matthew, then stared out at the crowded floor, his glasses already fogged with sweat.

"Things happen, Matthew. Things happen. I guess they figured no point holding me for getting rid of a cat like Tommy. I probably did 'em a favor."

Matthew felt his throat tighten and remnants of the dream came back.

"Tommy was my friend, Rhino."

Rhino shrugged, his face expressionless in the dim light. He fumbled in his pocket and threw a dirty, crumpled bill on the counter. "Gordon's straight up."

Blue moved to the center of the bar, leaned against the back wall and folded his arms across his chest. "Not in here. Not tonight. Not never!!"

The music had stopped completely now and Blue's voice, hoarse with anger, carried through the thick silence. "Not never, mothafucka. Tommy was my ace."

Scattered murmurs from the dancers: "You tell 'im, Blue!"

"That's right. He blow Tommy away and come back now acting like nothing happened."

Rhino turned from the bar and faced the darkened dance floor, his eyes darting like pinpoints behind his glasses. A second passed and he turned again and placed his hands on the bar. Matthew stared at his face, ridged with scars. He looked at the thin, colorless fingers and the lost dream came into focus. He saw the knife coming down again.

"So that's the way it's gonna be?" Rhino asked no one in particular, scanning the bandstand.

"That's the way it's gonna be 'cause that's the way it is," Blue said, stepping forward to lean on the bar. The sleeves of his yellow silk shirt were rolled up revealing arms carved like old oak. He laced his fingers and waited.

Rhino picked up the bill from the counter and balled it in his fist. "Well, we gonna see about that. Tommy got what was coming and I still got some business to finish."

"Well you ain't hardly finishing it in here, "Blue said, reaching under the counter. "Don't disgrace the place with your face. Git the fuck on out!"

Matthew quickly stepped out of range as Blue came up with his .38 and took aim. The dancers came to life and scattered.

Some piled into the tiny rest room. Others jammed into the coat check room. The musicians abandoned their instruments and ran for the narrow, make-shift kitchen, nearly trampling the cook.

"See what I mean, Rhino. Your pasty pink ass ain't on the scene a hot second and already your shit done hit the fan."

Blue rested the gun loosely in the crook of his arm and motioned toward the door again. "So like I said, take your ass the hell on outta here!"

Rhino backed away from the bar, and from the nervous laughter. The crowd had emerged again now that Blue had everything under control.

At the door, he turned again, causing a few of the patrons to shift and melt into the shadows but Matthew, against his will, had edged through the crowd, drawn by the expression on Rhino's face and the scars that had not been there when he left.

Behind the thick glasses, Matthew read the earlier history and for a moment, something inside him paused. He remembered the day, years ago, when the boy's fifteen year old mother had stared at the colorless infant and walked out of the hospital and out of his life. Didn't linger long enough to even give him a name. His grandmother had brought him home.

And on a Sunday six months later, Reverend Sister Marthie had baptized him in her 8th Avenue Storefront Temple of Heavenly Light because the priest at the regular church, not finding a father's name on the birth certificate, had refused.

...We all chipped in for the baptism and for the party afterward. We even bought his outfit. But after that, it was one thing, then another. School lasted just long enough for him to find his way out the door and outrun the other names. His grandma tried, but her face stayed in a puff. Lids half mast from all the crying. It was one damn thing after another.

Matthew was never quite certain when the rage had crawled inside the boy but he and everyone else knew when it began to creep out. He remained silent now as he gazed at the ruined face, the rumpled jacket hanging from the wire thin frame and the too-large pants cuffs draped around Rhino's shoes. He stared into the clouded glasses as Rhino opened his hand and let the bill fall to the floor.

"Here you go, Blue..You gonna need this."

Then he turned in the silence and disappeared through the door held open for him. Matthew followed through the corridor to overtake him, to ask what he intended by the remark.

...If he planning on toasting the joint, at least be man enough to say so. So we could be on the lookout and...

But Rhino had already approached the stairs and, as Matthew watched, seemed to float through the darkness like a wraith, as if the steps did not exist for him.

Matthew reacted as if a cold front had moved in, enveloping him, displacing the weight of the night heat.

He backed away.

At the bar, Blue had a double Cutty Sark waiting.

"What you think, Matt?" Blue said, pushing the drink toward Matthew before filling another glass for himself. He had not had to pull the piece in quite a while and Rhino's sudden appearance now caused his hand to shake.

Matthew shrugged and sipped the drink through a straw to avoid aggravating his sore chops. He listened to the pianist glide through an Errol Garner riff, trying to recapture the mood but the feeling had evaporated, replaced now by a fine tension that held everyone's eyes toward the door.

Matthew drank quickly and signaled for a refill.

"Can't figure out how he's out so soon," Blue said. "Supposed to do ten and out in two don't make sense unless he cut a deal, ratted out somebody in the joint. Yeah, that's it. And he got enough scars to scare the hell out of a blind man."

"It don't matter how or why," Matthew said. "Point is, he's back and a lot madder than when he left..."

He glanced at his watch. "Hell, it's one a.m. If it wasn't so late, I'd wake up every damn body in the building, just to pull their coat."

Blue wiped the counter and glanced at the thinning crowd. Most people were heading toward the door.

"Don't think about the clock, man. Folks already got the wire.

"I've been in 1048 long enough to know how the news seeps in through the bricks and plaster. Come up through the radiators if it's bad enough."

Matthew nodded and placed his glass on the counter.

...Blue's right. I woke up in that sweat, should've known some bad news was around the corner. Old folks say: fish fry, birds fly, and one thing, Baby, is dreams don't lie. Tell you everything you need to know. Especially if you don't want to know it. Should've been on my P's and Q's from the jump.

The musicians gathered their instruments and had drawn a faded quilt over the piano. "What's happening tomorrow?" the bassist asked, glancing at the chair Rhino had kicked over.

"Same time, same station," Matthew said, before Blue could answer.

"Yeah, see y'all tomorrow," Blue nodded, looking around the now empty room.

...Hell with it. Can't let Rhino throw a hammer in. The joint is cool, and not too far to go if anybody get himself too tight to navigate, which hardly happens. And the Jazz Net. Style ain't exactly the Modern Jazz Quartet, but they bring in the folks who don't mind letting the eagle fly. Last night was a slammer, and tonight woulda been alright too, but...

He let out a sigh and watched Matthew remove the mouthpiece from the sax and place the instrument in its case. He was too quiet..

"So what you think?" he asked again.

Matthew moved his shoulders slightly. "I don't know. Maybe he was cut loose because everybody knows a black life don't count for nothing. Just one more black man getting rid of another. No big deal. And now he's out to maybe do more damage. I don't know. Maybe he was just talking trash. "

But as Matthew snapped the case shut, his mind was racing. ...what shit does Rhino have to finish. He was always strange, like he only ate nails for breakfast but no one figured he would actually ice somebody. And least of all, Tommy. Who is he after now? Could be any one of us. Maybe it's Rose. Every time he got near her, he breathed like a rock was stuck in his throat.

Or it could be her uncle, Cyrus. Or maybe it's Effie. Shit. In the dream, it was me!

He paused at the door to watch Blue brush the plastic cups from the table into a large cardboard carton. Next, Blue would stack the chairs, clean the floor, and then tally up for the night.

"Want me to hang around?"

"Naw. I got Betsy here. On my hip with a full clip. She'll see me to my pad. If anything goes down, we are ready."

Matthew opened the door and gazed out into the corridor. Night had washed away all dimension and he could see nothing. Despite the years he had been coming here, he still could not tell if the passageway was long, short, narrow, or wide.

More than once, he had listened to some of the regulars, after a few drinks, debate whether the alley existed at all. They just seemed to float through it, they said, not feeling walls, ceiling, or floor.

...But those were the hooch hounds, the wide mouthed, two drinks-a-minute guys. .Elbows up and heads to the side, downing gin like they thought prohibition was coming back.

And Matthew was usually sober when he stepped into the corridor leading to the alley. He moved blind, with faith tapping like a walking stick.

He had once asked Blue why he didn't put a light in the corridor and Blue had looked at him, surprised that he hadn't figured it out.

"I'd have to change the name, man. Alley wouldn't be blind no more. Besides, folks just kind of follow the music, you know. The sound is their guide."

Matthew finally closed the door and tried to imagine this scene through Rhino's defective vision and his all-encompassing anger.

...Hell with this. Gotta have a serious converse with everybody in the place. The sooner the better.

He moved carefully, holding the horn in its case against his chest. The rain had stopped and in the silence, the alley closed in. He heard the scratching sound again and paused in the indefinable darkness, listening. A minute later, he moved forward, deciding that the sound had come from the beating of his own heart.

Chapter Two
APT 2A

"I waited up," Sandra said as Matthew placed the case on the kitchen table. It was 2 a.m. and beyond the closed door down the hall, Matthew could hear Theo's muffled snores. He envied the boy.

"Don't tell me you heard the news already," Matthew said as he sat and removed his tie and shirt.

Sandra poured another cup of coffee and pushed it across the table. *What news? Had the Alley been raided? Had anyone been arrested? All that money Blue paid the cops to keep things quiet…*

What news?" she whispered, trying to keep her voice steady. Matthew tried to glance away but failed. "Rhino's back," he said finally.

Sandra searched his face. Surely he was joking.

"It's true, Sandy. He came in the Alley about an hour ago. Busted right in and started selling wolf tickets. Blue called his hand and he faded. Probably across the way right now plotting how he's gonna get even…"

Sandra placed her cup in the saucer and folded her arms on the table. She looked around the small kitchen as if seeing it for the first time. It was clean and orderly and received so much sunlight that a tiny pot of ivy, a mother's day gift, had spread like a cool green picture frame thickly around the window. And Theo had teased her: "Well, I guess we won't be moving anywhere. Can't cut Mom loose from that plant."

Matthew had felt tired when he turned the key in the door and hoped Sandra would have been asleep. All he had wanted was to tip in, ease into bed next to her and wake up when he felt that satin night gown curl around her legs. And any news about Rhino could have waited until morning.

Her brown face was framed by sand colored hair and her deep set eyes were now clouded. Matthew usually thought of dark pools each time he gazed at her. Now she had that look that said they needed to talk.

He drank his coffee too quickly, scalding and further aggravating his already sore mouth. "Listen, Sandy, if anybody has to go, it's not gonna be us. If we didn't move when Theo was born, why should we do it now?"

Matthew thought of all the folks in the house, the conversations he enjoyed with Cyrus: the aroma that filled the hallway around Thanksgiving when Effie started to bake her holiday fruitcakes. And Rose, flighty as she was, could really put a Christmas party together. The Morgans were newcomers who mostly kept to themselves so he couldn't judge them one way or the other. And now, to have to move, leave all the poker games up on tar beach, and all his guys down in the Alley, the music and the good times.

He shook his head. "Well, maybe Rhino was bad back then, but we didn't move because.."

" – because he didn't commit murder?" Sandra asked. She waved her finger lightly, like a schoolteacher, whenever she corrected anyone. "You must've forgotten that little boy down the block…Seaweed?"

Matthew went silent, then rubbed his face. "Jesus, how could I forget? Yeah, that-"

Sandra rose from the table, went to the sink and splashed water noisily in her cup before Matthew could begin to talk. She had her own memories and did not want to hear another's.

*** ***

Seaweed – everyone had forgotten his given name– was Marcella's son. She did not live on the block but hung out on 7th Avenue in the bar with her sister. When she found she was pregnant, her sister suggested that salt, lots of it would take care of the problem.

Marcella drank a gallon of salt water and two pints of Night Train a day. Nevertheless, she carried to term, had a normal delivery, and took to hanging out again as if nothing extraordinary had happened.

But the child –nicknamed Seaweed by the sister who had advised Marcella to take all that salt water in the first place –was a bit slow. At eight years of age, he had walked, talked, and arrived at conclusions with great difficulty. And he was drawn to Rhino who was two years older because no one else seemed interested in making the important decisions in his life.

But Rhino was jealous. Slow as Seaweed was, neglected and ragged as he was, he at least had a mother. Rhino was eaten with envy the few times he had seen Marcella actually talk to Seaweed: when she had patted the boy on his uncombed head and given him a dime for a frankfurter which all three knew would be his only meal until the next morning when she returned home, red-eyed and linty-haired, walking fast, trying to control the dangerous list in her stroll.

But when she handed the coin to her son, every curl was in place and Rhino inhaled the volatile scent of Evening In Paris crème sachet. "Y'all be good," she smiled, "I'm coming right back" which all three knew was an unnecessary lie.

"I'm coming right back." The phrase danced in Rhino's imagination. His own mother had never said that to him.

Or anyone. Instead, he imagined that she had pulled back that hospital blanket down to his knees to make sure God's anger hadn't stopped at the neck, drew her breath at the sight of his colorless skin, and walked quickly out of the ward.

..Never even held him, never given him a dime for a frankfurter but left in her void a grandmother, once removed by age and attitude, who had never quite reached through the curtain of her own grief to truly touch him. Her daughter- his mother's- absence was a presence in the house that smothered him, made him cry out and repeat the fast, cold phrases he'd heard the slick corner men use. He hadn't understood, but when he looked in the eyes of their women, he knew that the words had the power to break stone. He absorbed the sounds, combinations of them, and in the midnight hour, screamed them at his mother's shadow and hoped he had made her cry.

He took charge of Seaweed. He invented their schemes and games – the favorite being 'hit the beam', which they played in the shadow of the 8th Avenue elevated line, in that vague one minute, half light just before true night closed in, just before a driver thought to turn on his headlights.

The two boys crouched behind the steel girders, and then one dashed out at the last second to disappear behind another girder. The car usually swerved to avoid the child, and the driver would scream 'get the heck out of the street. Are you nuts?'

They took turns – that is, Seaweed usually dashed three times to Rhino's one, to prove, Rhino said, 'since you so slow, you got to do it more times to show you just as quick."

Sandra had been walking from the A&P, struggling to keep her coat fastened over her stomach and glad that Bennie, the clerk, was available to help her carry the groceries. The crowd at the intersection had blocked traffic and a sound drifted above it, mournful and senseless in its fright.

"What happened? What is it?"

"Kid got hit."

"Who? Who?" Sandra asked, not wanting to know.

The mournful sounds took shape…"Maaaa…"

Bennie put down the package, worked his way through the crowd and came back, shaking his head. "I knew it. I knew it had to be one of 'em, Mrs. Paige. Had to be one of 'em sooner or later."

"Who?" Sandra asked again, not wanting to know but too frightened not to know.

She made up her mind. … When this baby comes, we're moving. We're not staying in this city another day. All these fast cars..

"It's Seaweed," Bennie said. "Buick got him good. But he ain't dead yet. They're still trying to get him in the ambulance. Too bad it wasn' t that damn – pardon me Mrs. Paige- but too bad it wasn't that Rhino. He was always egging that boy on. Knowin' he ain't too bright . And look what happened. Look what happened."

Sandra felt a sudden ache- though she wasn't due for another five weeks. The lower part of her stomach started to squeeze and her swollen legs felt like granite.

… Rhino. This was bound to happen. Always bullying that child, laughing at his clumsiness…

"Maaaa…"

The sound ebbed, and then flowed away into the half-light leaving a silence that pressed against Sandra. She needed to sit down. On the ground. Or in that ambulance. Night had come out of nowhere, thick, quick, blotting away faces and leaving gray, shifting outlines of curious onlookers.

Just then, she felt that if Marcella had shown up, wobbling on her thin high heels and skinny, knotted legs she would have found the strength and a big stick to beat her into the ground.

Another sensation, hot, insistent, washing up toward her navel. She needed to sit down.

"Bennie, listen. I'm…I'm not.."

She dropped the one package she had been carrying and leaned heavily on his arm. "Oh. Just get me home. Please, Bennie.."

"Mrs. Paige…do you want...I can't..."

Bennie, panicked, had bent down, trying to retrieve the packages as Sandra clung to him.

"Lady? You need help?" A voice had detached itself from the gray huddle.

"She shouldn't be looking at none of this," someone else whispered. "Might mark the baby."

But it was too late. The crowd had parted and Sandra glimpsed in the headlights of the ambulance the bloodstained girder and the shreds of grayish corduroy stuck to it. She also spied Rhino skirting the edge of the crowd, his thin yellow arms folded above his head as if to protect himself from an anticipated blow, moving slowly, his face completely without expression.

She needed to sit down.

"C'mon, mister. We help you. This your wife? Take it easy, m'am. Things gonna be all right. You gonna be fine…"

And three strong men, along with Bennie, brought her home and managed to get her with her swollen legs and stomach up the stairs and Matthew opened the door and nearly fainted.

In the ambulance, they strapped her to the narrow stretcher because she could not stop twisting and turning . Her hair had come undone and her clothing clung to her in a vapor of sweat.

"..Is there blood, Matthew? Is there blood?"

"What? Sandra, I don't-"

The attendant wiped her face with Matthew's handkerchief. "No, mother, there's only water. Your water broke, that's all. That's natural. You're going to be all right."

But Sandra twisted and turned, trying to look at the floor or at least the shaking walls and when she cried out, she said 'Poor baby. Poor boy. Poor boy."

Frightening Matthew all the more because he did not understand how his wife could know she was going to have a boy and why it should be doomed to be poor and he felt his own tears because maybe she was right that he should have gotten a decent job sooner instead of playing those damn dead-end gigs and now she wouldn't be going through so much pain if only he could've made her happier and if she didn't pull through this he would get a gun and blow his brains out and he held her head and pressed her damp forehead as the ambulance rattled through the changing lights.

He never heard the mournful siren because he cried and cried as Sandra twisted and turned trying to see the floor, to see if a bit of Seaweed was there.

*** ***

Sandra came home ten days later and told Matthew what she had seen. The baby, Theo, born prematurely, came home twenty one days later. Seaweed returned home sixty days after.

And Rhino thought long and hard and decided there was nothing much he could do with a leg-less boy in a creaky wheelchair so he simply forgot about him.

Later, long after the elevated structure had been torn down, finally bathing the peddlers' carts that lined 8th Avenue in brilliant, unfamiliar, sunlight; and children playing hopscotch were able to see their shadows on the pavement, and long after the small A&P with its fresh ground coffee fragrance had abandoned the neighborhood, and after Seaweed had died from all the infections that just kept coming back and everyone had forgotten even his nickname, Sandra remembered and harbored a deep and abiding hatred for Rhino.

When he had been sent to prison for killing Tommy, she had hoped it would be for life.

Chapter Three

APT 2B

Fannie Dillard turned from the stove.

"How come you didn't let me know you were getting out?"

"Didn't think it mattered," Rhino answered.

"One way or the other, you'd know I was back."

He moved the can of beer from his mouth and looked at his grandmother. Her skin was smooth and dark and highlighted the curve of perspiration near her mouth. Her hair was plaited in one long braid that reached past her shoulders. She looked healthier, not fat, but more substantial than he remembered.

The familiar cotton bathrobe had faded a bit and the bend in her shoulders seemed more pronounced. He watched her hands which seemed to move with an old nervousness.

"What's wrong? You ain't glad to see me?"

Fannie Dillard did not answer. She tried not to look at him but instead gazed at the scraps of food on the table around the empty plate, the scattered stains, and the rings from the beer cans settling into the white linen tablecloth.

"It's not that," she said finally. "You know it's not that. It's just that I didn't expect you so soon and also you said that when you got out, you were gonna look for someplace else to settle in. You weren't coming back here."

She avoided looking directly at him but watched his colorless fingers toy with the now empty beer can, spinning it around on the table so that the few remaining drops sprayed out, further soiling the cloth.

"Well, I kinda changed my mind."

"Changed your - but you said- "

"I know what I said. This is only gonna be temporary."

"How temporary?"

"Temporary. That's all I can say right now."

He tried to make it sound important, this temporary visit, as if he had some major business to attend during this interval.

But Fannie Dillard knew better. She moved toward the sink, knowing that temporary was a sometime thing. A day. A lifetime. For her, it had meant more than twenty years of her life since her daughter, Audrey, had taken one look at the boy's skin and decided that he didn't belong to her. Left him there in the hospital and disappeared.

The last rumor Fannie had been able to track down was of Audrey shaking a tambourine in a south Bronx choir, having been saved, it was said, by a holiness preacher and wanting nothing to do with her former fast life.

Everyone in 1048 suspected the super, Drunken Lee Brown, was the father of the child since he also disappeared the day Fannie brought the baby home. Audrey had been only fifteen and Drunken Brown would have gone to jail. She, Fannie, would have seen to it.

She named the child Richard though few people aside from the police knew that. And she slipped in 'Lee' as his middle name just in case Drunken Brown, in old age and finally sober, returned to acknowledge the boy and maybe set things halfway right.

She did not know when that other name had been tied on him. 'Rh'ino.' It sounded hard, like the skin of that ugly animal. Richard. Albino. 'bino. Then combined and shortened and simplified. Easier to tease though she had pretended not to hear the stunning cruelty of the children.

'Bino, bino what we gonna do.
Get a little paint and
Turn you black and blue

Or the devastating force of the 'the dozens'
'Rh'ino Rh'ino
Ain't you heard
No good daddy

Drinks thunderbird
Rh'ino Rh'ino
Ain't you heard
Mama skipped town
And never said a word.

...All it did was make him mean. Fought from the time he was able to make a fist. Always wanting to defend himself against stuff he never even understood. And still don't. Maybe Tommy had teased him too. Who knows? Tommy's dead and all my prayers ain 't gonna undo nuthin'.

The boy just needs to get away from here. Put some distance between himself and all this mess.

She washed the dish and wanted to remove the tablecloth, maybe put some lemon or at least some vinegar on the stains, but decided to wait until he went to bed.

...First night back, no point in upsetting him more. Just come in and seems like something's gotten to him already. I can see it. And all those scars. Must have been fighting from the time those gates closed on him. God, what am I supposed to do now? I tried my best. What more can I do?

Several seconds passed in which she wanted to go to him and put her arms around his thin shoulders as she had done so many times and tell him that everything was going to be all right. It was going to be all right. But she allowed the moment to pass and in the silence wondered again how he felt, having murdered a man.

Finally, she said, 'it's three a.m. and you need some shut eye after that long ride."

He shrugged but did not look at her and she left him sitting at the table.

In her bedroom, she quietly turned the lock and leaned against the door. Her heart was racing too fast and if she lay down, she was afraid she might not wake up.

...God, what can I do? All I ever wanted was some peace. That's not asking too much. Never could figure what was on that boy's mind. Everything he did was so...confusing. Like telling people that his mama was in Hollywood, a big dancer, wearing jewels and looking pretty and all, like that bird over the bar. Wrote those little post cards to himself and scrawled her name.

Even the post man felt sorry for him.

Then telling everybody that she was down south and coming for him any day. Then, her being sick and couldn't come back just yet. When he said she had died in a car crash, I just couldn't take any more. Not another, lying, word.

She thought about it, remembering the splayed palm print purple-red on his face. The blow had spoken of her fatigue and hope and hopelessness; of changing and washing diapers, of teething pain, snotty noses, 3.a.m. colic, coughs, and fever; of resting her head for a quick minute on the kitchen table and waking to the smell of a burnt pot in which the baby formula had boiled away. It spoke of patiently teaching him to hold a spoon and to tie a shoe lace and of bundling him in her lap when he woke crying in the dark, and of sitting with him by the window scanning 8th avenue, studying the pattern of any young girl who seemed to walk pigeon-toed, like his mother.

The blow was meant to knock the lie out of him and remind him that her daughter. Was. Not. Dead.

Maybe lost. Maybe away for awhile but never, never to the point where she couldn't come back anymore.

The blow was about teaching him truth when she herself could not accept the truth.

...I hit him and he never did cry. Just stared at me...

She closed her eyes and tried to listen to her heartbeat. It had slowed but she was still afraid to lie down. Instead, she gathered up the coverlet from the bed and sat near the window. She drew back the blinds and adjusted the screen.

8th Avenue was deserted except for a couple standing on the corner. A cab pulled up and they entered. A light wind blew across the street now empty of sound. The silence was a blessing. She needed to think, not sleep.

...Temporary. Well, he came back for something, but whatever it is, I hope all those prison fights taught him a thing or two about knowing the difference between right and wrong. Something I could never get him to understand.

Chapter Four
RHINO

Rhino waited until he heard the turn of the lock, and then quietly began to search through the kitchen cabinets. There was no hidden bottle.

"...Must've stopped drinkin' when I left."

He settled for another can of beer from the refrigerator and paced the floor as he drank.

"Never should've come back. Should've headed straight to the Coast. Everybody in the joint braggin' how it's easy there. Don't even need keys. Everything's open. Just walk right in."

He bent the can between his fingers. "That's what I'll do. Don't even unpack . "

He stared at the suitcase that held his few belongings. The bag was small and cheaply made and the lock had sprung open, broken even before he had boarded the train from Elmira.

At Grand Central, he had thought of throwing it away, discarding everything in it all at once and buying new socks and underwear and anything that did not have the stale odor of prison soap dried into it. But he had been given fifty eight dollars and the train ticket. In the two years, he had earned fifty eight dollars, the only money he had ever worked for in his 24 years.

He dug into his pocket and brought out the crumpled bills.

"Old lady be glad to double this, just to get me out of here. But I gotta see about something."

Earlier, when he had taken the bus uptown from Grand Central, a light rain had fallen and the fine mist clung to the windows causing everything outside to blur past in a dull yellow streak of lighted store fronts. Now and then, an umbrella-d silhouette flashed in dark relief but he had neither wondered nor cared who they were. He had held only the image of Rose before him.

There had been nothing but mist in the street when he had stepped off the bus, mist and the flashing neon of the Peacock Bar.

"I should've gone in the bar. Maybe she was there, but –"

He lined up the empty beer cans on the table, stacked them one atop the other, and then knocked them all down.

"...instead, I went into the Alley and let Matthew and Blue jump bad. And everybody else stuck their two cents in."

He glanced at the wall clock. "I could maybe ease up and knock on her door but maybe she ain't even livin' here no more."

A pressure in his head seemed to spread as he stared at the wall clock fashioned in the shape of a smiling cat. Its glass eyes ticked back and forth and the curled tail moved like a pendulum.

Fannie Dillard had put that clock away to keep him from destroying it.

"Thought I wasn't comin' back. The old lady. Matthew. Rose. Everybody."

He began to pace in the small space again.

"Don't need to see no wild west just yet. Only one did the most talkin' about it is pullin' a thirty to life bid. Stick here for a while, least till I get my business straight. And ain't nuthin' nobody can do about it. Fuck 'em all.

He swept a beer can up from the table and squinted at the ticking clock.

*** ***

Years ago, he had found the photograph, wrapped in cellophane, and hidden at the bottom of the closet under several folded quilts. He had brought it out, propped it against the lamp on the chest, taken the magnifying glass stolen long ago from the 5&10 and began the familiar ritual.

The glass moved haltingly over the surface of the picture, enlarging the dark face of the fourteen year old girl trying hard to appear older. Her large, expressive eyes seemed to widen or narrow depending on the angle at which he held the glass.

The picture had been taken with an old Brownie and the white blouse and long plaid skirt with the pleats which seemed to move as he held the glass had faded to a monochromatic tan. The girl in the photo leaned against the stoop's iron railing, one hand holding a small kitten and the other waving in the airy style of a movie star embarking on an ocean liner.

Sailing away. Bon voyage, she waved.

His head began to ache again.

She had said goodbye even before she had taken that step into that unknown bed.

Bon voyage.

He studied the face, searching the pores in her dark skin for connection and wondering why there had to be this vast difference which everyone in the neighborhood and the world was only too glad to let him know in ugly rhythm and rhyme.

He studied the cat in the photo and wondered what had happened to that particular one. He knew what had happened to the others that came after, until his grandmother finally paid attention to the rumors and decided he was capable of doing what they said he did and took care not to bring any more pets into the house.

Bon voyage.

What did I do to you except get born? Wasn't my fault. I didn 't ask. And I bet you took that fuckin' cat. That goddamn smelly fuckin' cat.

He spread his fingers wide over the photo so that the girl's face was framed in the V of his thumb and forefinger. He compared the brown against the pink and began the familiar litany of hatred because the pink never got any darker no matter how often he did it.

Bon voyage.

Her thin arms remained in the air and he stared at the picture until the image blurred.

Chapter Five

APT 2A

"What a difference a day makes… twenty four little…"

Matthew Paige hummed as his son practiced. "Wait. Start again, Theo. Slower. And hold your fingers like.."

Theo watched his father take the clarinet and position it just above his lower lip. Matthew flexed his fingers and the melody floated lightly through the room. Sound ebbed and flowed around the sofa, the Philco console, and circled the upright piano which Matthew had had hauled up the two stories on a creaking winch last summer.

The clarinet moved between Matthew 's fingers like a wand and pressed Theo into a respectful silence. He knew if he played all his life, he could never produce this elusive harmony or the resonant chords that made him want to cry.

At 15, Theo was nearly six feet, almost as tall as his father. He had his father's smooth features, large eyes, and strong jaw – a face many of the girls in school called handsome. When he smiled his teeth were bright and even.

He rested against the sill near the open window and listened to the melody, wondering how his father made it seem so easy. As far back as he could remember, and before he knew how the notes emerged from the bell of a horn, there was the image of his father, the musician standing tall and lean and wide legged, eyes squinted tight and jaws like a blowfish, making the sax speak to the walls in a language that he, Theo, had been too young to understand.

Now at fifteen, he was no closer to understanding but just as determined to speak that same way with his clarinet.

Matthew extended the instrument. "Here. Let's see what you can do."

Theo began again and this time, Matthew closed his eyes.

Boy's sounding real good. Stuff coming as natural as breathing... maybe..

Theo hit an off note and Matthew winced.

"Try it one more once," he said, his eyes still closed.

Theo shifted his position on the window sill. "Yeah, I heard that one myself.."

He began again and Matthew's thoughts, against his will, began to drift.

Can't see Rhino turning up. Like a damn bad penny. Seems like he would've pointed himself in some other direction and kept on stepping.

He checked his watch again.

Three o'clock. Cyrus won't be home for another hour. Time enough to tell him then, if he hasn't already found out. Right now, this boy's technique could use some fine tuning.

He held up his hand, palm down, - like a conductor. "Slow it. Don't rush. Concentrate on the low, the slow. Once more now..."

And he listened to a tapestry of sound, woven note upon note, as his son filled the room with silken melody. Theo leaned near the sill of the half opened window, his back to the courtyard as he played and Matthew knew that each note was shaped to catch in the updraft and float like a fine particle on a sunbeam. The note would play against the busy clotheslines, then make its way up and up and glide through the window of apartment 3B

Theo was not practicing. He was entertaining Sara Morgan as she did her homework.

...If I look up quick, Matthew thought, I could probably catch that small ripple in her living room curtain. She does that to let him know she's listening. When he sees that curtain move, he becomes a regular pied piper. Ah, what the hell. No need to embarrass 'em. God bless young love but thank God for smart parents. Can't be tight enough on these kids nowadays. Boy's got plenty of time later to think about romance. Only fifteen – nearly sixteen – and hasn't said a word about college yet. In fact, he's hardly opened a book since that girl moved in the house.

Matthew remembered the one time Sara had come to visit- -her mother, polite but hawk-eyed--was with her. And Theo had showed Sara how to hold a flute. Her fingers were long and slender, better suited to the violin, but she had smiled and asked questions and had Theo walking in a trance for a month.

...the girl's family has plans for her. Wants her to go to medical school and she's in line for a scholarship. Meanwhile, she's got this boy's head turned every way but straight. He cracks a book only when his mother starts yelling. Me and him got to have another talk. He's got to be ready. It's not like when I was comin' up. Now the Supreme Court say you can go to any damn school you want. Any school you want. Ain't that something? And I'm gonna see that he does.

Theo hit a particularly high note, held it, and then segued into a series of soft riffs. Matthew listened for several minutes before he nodded. "Good! That's it. You got it."

Theo was sweating when he put the clarinet down. He knew he would have to work harder on his breathing but he had sounded pretty good and he knew that Sara had heard him.

"So it was all right?"

"It was all right, Theo, but you want to be more than all right. Music comes to you naturally. You don't have to struggle with it but I want to see you get serious about school work. You have to open those books for more than half an hour –"

Theo pretended to listen as he fitted the clarinet into its velvet lined case – a gift from his mother last Christmas. Why couldn't his father pay a compliment without wrapping it in a half hour lecture about his study habits. He resisted the urge to shape his mouth to follow his father's words.

-you kids today have opportunities I never even dreamed of when I was your age...

...Right on line. Not one word off. Not one syllable. I can repeat it better than he can.

Theo straightened up. His smile was genuine even though his father got on his nerves at times. "I'm gonna try, Dad. And music might help pay my way through law school – "

...Law school. Did I hear right? He started to smile but checked himself. Where had this idea come from? Had the girl mentioned she liked lawyers?

"Now that's news," he said cautiously. "How'd you decide on that?"

"Thurgood Marshall," Theo said, placing the case near the piano. "Since he argued before the Court and won, all the guys want to be like him. That's all we talk about now."

Matthew listened, barely able to contain himself. This was wonderful. Now he'd have Cyrus speak to the boy, impress on him the importance of study, hard study. After all, Cyrus had a degree in history and everyone in the house looked up to him.

The room was quiet after Theo left except for the click of the metronome. He could have reached up and turned it off but the beat kept his mind from wandering.

My old man always said each generation should be at least one step ahead of the last one. That's what keeps the race moving. This boy has got to do better than me... That girl just got here and already she and her folks know which way she's gonna go.

Matthew loved his wife and son, and music was the air he breathed, yet he had ended up in the Post Office in a deadly secure clerk's job where his dreams had dried and blown away in the canvas avalanche of heavy gray mail sacks.

He lit a cigarette and allowed himself to drift with the mood though not necessarily wanting to acknowledge the passage of time and the weight of his failed dreams.

When he was younger, he had wanted most of all to play in the Basie band. He had wanted to be a member of that elite group who had jammed the Apollo, stomped down the Savoy, and blew the roof off the clubs in Paris.

And later, when swing gave way to bop, he had dreamed of going toe to toe with J.J. Johnson and Kai Windig as they laid Newport low.

Everyone knew he was good – more than good- but the bands, as big as they were, could accommodate only so many. The smaller groups he joined to assuage his disappointment all dissolved under the rigors of one night stands, crooked booking agents, cheating women and that bad new monkey that had climbed so easily onto the backs of so many sidemen.

But music was what he knew and he carried the sound of this knowledge to Chicago and Kansas and Detroit and all the small, packed, Elks clubs in between.

And one night, he heard the voice of this woman singing in her kitchen next door to the only rooming house open to the colored in this nameless Tennessee town he'd passed through.

(To spend one night with you…)

He had played three sets back to back with only a ten minute break at a combination rib joint/dance hall where the crowd, starved for blues and boogie, had turned raucous, and the club owner threatened to not pay any musician who dared step off the stage.

(…In our own rendezvous…)

His chops were sore and his feet were so swollen, he could barely stand and he had been glad to see the tiny two dollar bed.

(…that's my desire..)

A-cappella sound drifting like snowflakes on the night air, floating through the cedar and shingle. He lay under the tattered quilt listening and wondering if notes had colors and what color were the ones drifting toward him.

(…to spend one night with you…)

…Snow covered notes, frozen in glittering shape.

No, not exactly frozen when they reached his ears, but swollen with a loneliness that moved him from under the quilt and caused him to slip and slide on the thin layer of ice covering the narrow walkway between the two houses.

He tapped on the door, having no idea what she would look like, no idea if she was married and whether a big, country, bruiser of a husband would answer his timid knock and lay him out cold.

She answered the door herself, gave him a long look, and pressed her small hand to her chest. "For heaven's sake, come in before you catch your death out there."

Her small brown face framed by sand colored hair matched the symmetry of her voice. He gazed at her, open-mouthed, and in that instant, the idea and habit of one night stands blew away on the frigid air.

Sixteen years ago. 1938. Had he really stood speechless and shivering on that porch that night? And had he really worked non-stop in order to send that bus ticket?

Three months later, she had been the last to step off the Greyhound, the curve of her smile bracketed by a kind of mute terror which only slightly dissipated when they reached Harlem.

He saw this and so they did not go directly to 1048. Instead, they had dinner at Tante Beryl's Creole Restaurant, and then walked the length of Lenox Avenue. He felt her valise gain weight with each block so he finally guided her into the dark and noisy atmosphere of the Club Baron on 132nd Street where everyone knew him and would, if he was lucky, attest to his sterling character.

At the bar, the crowd huddled around the tiny radio.

"Any wagers? I'm takin' on all comers," someone yelled.

The fight between Louis and Schmelling was about to begin.

"Bets are off," Matthew answered as he led Sandra to a table near the bandstand where the musicians were setting up. "I know how it's gonna turn out. Not like last time."

"Yeah, but what round?"

"Who cares, as long as my boy knocks that kraut out," someone else volunteered.

"Well, I ain't so sure," a man at the table nearest Matthew said. "The Brown Bomber been slippin' lately. Too many women on his mind."

"Man, you talkin' heresy now."

"This ain't no hear-say. I know –"

" Listen," the bartender warned, "y'all got to take that talk for a walk. I want to hear when I win my money."

They were interrupted by the high metallic voice of the announcer.

Schmelling's on the ropes. Brown Bomber's closing in. Schmelling's covering up. Louis has found the opening he needs! Going for the kill! Pounding! A right to the head. A left uppercut to the jaw. Schmelling's knees are gone! He's down! He's down!

The roar of the stadium crowd, sounding like so much static on the small radio, was drowned out by the bar crowd.

"Louis! Joe Louis! Two minutes…first round."

The gamblers and drinkers wheeled off the bar stools and rushed to the street. The musicians, with their instruments, abandoned the stage and followed. All around them was noise.

Matthew looked at Sandra. "What do you say we step on out and join 'em?" he shouted.

She stared at him, wide eyed, as he stashed her valise under the table. The crowds on Lenox Avenue had stopped traffic. People poured into the street, banging on pots and pans, blowing whistles, clapping, screaming, "Brown Bomber! Brown Bomber!"

Joe Louis had won. And people could dance and sing and hug perfect strangers and forget about the Depression that had them by the throat; forget those soup kitchens where each time they served them a meal, there was a newsman in their face telling them to frown while he angled his camera for the ugliest shot - as if he didn't know some folks, born into this vale of tears- came here frowning.

And people could forget that half a world away Germany had swallowed Austria and was enlarging its appetite to ingest all of Europe. That meant nothing. Joe Louis, the Brown Bomber, had dusted a German right here in New York City, New York.

Strips of newspaper and precious rolls of toilet tissue arced from the roof tops, spinning out like rockets against the night sky.

At 125th Street, dancers jitterbugged ankle deep in home –made confetti.

Matthew and Sandra trailed the musicians, block after block, and finally back to the club where the celebration was in full swing.

Sandra, still wide-eyed, clapped as the vibes player stretched a twenty minute solo. Matthew hardly heard a note. He swallowed two drinks and forgot about the character confirmation. He dipped to one knee, reached for her hand, and formally proposed.

*** ***

A year after they were married, she said, "we have a baby on the way. You need to have a job, sugar…"

…Which had astounded him. All those times he had played at Atlantic City and Peg Leg Bates resort, (he never traveled far any more) and all the weddings and dances at the Park Palace on 110th street, the Golden Gate ballroom on Lenox, the Rockland Palace under the viaduct on 155th Street and at the Savoy Ballroom, he thought he *had* been working.

He said nothing, finally understanding what his father meant years ago when he had warned that love had peculiar powers. Especially when it's new.

Son, it can turn a rock to powder. Make milk look like ink. It can make a strong man hear himself say 'yes' when all he meant was 'maybe.'

Before Matthew understood this, he had laid his horn aside and was hoisting 100 pound sacks on the swing shift at the Post Office.

Now he listened to the metronome and watched the cigarette smoke spiral slowly to the ceiling. He remembered the crowded dance halls and all the after hours spots. He thought of the rent parties with the seven watt blue lights and loud Louis Jordan records. Quarter a shot whisky at a kitchen bar and pigs feet and red rice on the stove. And small time hustlers who everyone knew were busted, disgusted and not to be trusted because the only thing they had to spend was time.

He only played in a combo at those places. Three men at the most, who could move fast when a fist flew or the whistle blew. When the joint got hot, nobody stuck around to help the drummer pack. You could only wave as you scrambled down the fire escape.

Matthew crushed the cigarette in the ashtray and glanced around the cluttered living room. The music stand, slightly lopsided under the weight of the score sheets; the silent mahogany mass of the piano, and the delicate click of the metronome depressed him.

Last week, he'd read in *the Amsterdam* that two of his old sidemen had been hurt in a car accident on the way to a gig.

...Probably in a town so small, it was un-mappable. And now last night, the piano man said that Richie, who could make a bass speak in a language that ain't even been coined, Rich had got shot in a club in Baltimore.

Richie. Joe. Kenny. Old running buddies. Side kicks. Aces. Separated by miles of bad roads and lean years, yet still wedded, held together by their response to a peculiar rhythmic echo, that snap of the finger and tap of the toe when the lead man whispered, 'uh one and uh two and you know what to do.'

Time to jam.

...Well, the Alley's jumpin'. Not like those times, but hell, what is? Ain't that bad. But when word gets out that Rhino's on the scene, folks might want to gravitate someplace else no matter how good we sound.

He wrote a note for Sandra and propped it against the metronone. 'At Cyrus. Back in five.'

Chapter Six
APT 4B

Matthew watched Cyrus pace the length of the book-lined study, his hands clasped tightly behind him and his dark face creased in a frown. His beige linen suit was slightly wrinkled and his dense, gray streaked hair reminded Matthew of Frederick Douglass.

"I think we should tell Rose," Cyrus said. "Right away. From what you're saying, Matthew, I think Rhino came back for one purpose and that is to get even."

"Get even? With her? What did she ever do to him?"

Cyrus nodded but said nothing and Matthew thought he saw a hint of surprise.

Matthew remembered Rose, years earlier, when she had stepped onto the small stage in the Alley, with Cyrus urging her on. It had been a Wednesday night, slow time in the bars and even slower in the after hour spots so Blue had set up 'Amateur Hour in the Alley.'

The audience was loud and hard but anyone could get on stage for ten minutes and take his chances. If he kept the crowd happy without making a complete fool of himself, he was rewarded with a free bottle of 'might-be- champagne.'

Most of the contestants had more nerve than talent and that night Matthew remembered Rose's voice, for the first minutes, had wavered thin and frightened so he muted the horn and slowed the tempo and the musicians stayed with her. She was, after all, from 1048 and he wanted her to be good.

Guided by the softer sounds, her voice gained strength and seconds later, it flowed across the upturned faces in the dim and suddenly silent room,

...In the dark, in the dark
Just you and I
We gonna find
Ro..mance
In the dark

She had moved slowly behind the mike in a thin, yellow silk dress luminous against the dark background. Her pink wedgies had added three inches to her height and she appeared taller than her usual five feet five. Matthew remembered how the candlelight accented the loose curled hair, the half closed eyes and the thin wide mouth. Her tone, lighter and softer, became fine and mellow and pulled the crowd, against its will, to her.

Matthew wondered why, several months later, just as her voice was hitting its stride, she quit singing.

"What did your niece ever do to Rhino?" he asked again.

Cyrus remained quiet, wondering why Matthew had to ask. The first time Rose had stepped on stage and opened her mouth with that soft Hadda Brooks number, everyone had been taken by surprise, especially Tommy, the numbers banker, even though he had been sitting there with Babe, his girlfriend and business partner.

Cyrus, a table away, had watched the crowd's reaction: women glancing at their men as Rose closed her eyes and held the mike to her. The spotlight circled her dark face and she parted her mouth

...yes, we gonna find ro..mance
In the dar...ark...

Cyrus watched Tommy press a cigarette between his teeth and stare at Rose as if the two of them had been alone in the room.

He had also watched Rhino standing silently near the door staring as the crowd shared in Rose's noisy coronation .

He had shifted his attention from Tommy to Rhino and back again, wondering which one was staring the hardest at his niece.

Rose had once accused Cyrus of trying to place people under a microscope, 'to dissect them' she had said, 'like insects'. And he had shaken his head, appalled at the suggestion.

Perhaps. Because as much as he dissected, he never came up with clear answers. He wondered how Rose, her voice as soft and undefined as water, had held the crowd that night in the palm of her hand. He, himself, felt the vague, suggestive undertow of her power, but could not describe it, could not pinpoint it. When she left the stage with her prize, he had turned to the door again but the space Rhino had occupied was empty.

*** ***

It's not what Rose did," Cyrus said now as he filled Matthew's glass. "It's what she didn't do that's got Rhino so wound up."

Matthew put down the glass and waited. He had, when Cyrus offered 'a little treat to beat the heat', agreed to 'two fingers on the rocks', something to sip slowly just to be polite. But Cyrus poured bourbon like a bartender on a holiday, filling the glass to three quarters. To be polite, Matthew took a small sip and placed the glass on the coffee table. He scanned the floor-to-ceiling shelves of books and imagined the walls of Theo's law office looking like that one day.

Matthew had never met anyone quite like Cyrus. He had earned a degree in history but had worked as a red cap for years before finally getting the chance to teach, something he really wanted to do. Teach. But dreams have nightmare edges and now Cyrus had a lawsuit pending against the school system. Meanwhile, he sold insurance.

*** ***

Cyrus was forty two years old, and at five feet eleven, had the stocky muscularity of an athlete. His three piece suit looked cool and crisp even in August. Regardless of the weather, he walked the length and breadth of Harlem, his clients and former students greeting him as he passed. Even when he wasn't selling insurance, he walked.

"I've ridden enough trains to last a lifetime," he once said to Matthew. "Folks miss a lot when they're on wheels. Walking slows you down and allows time to take in life's details, the small things."

As a redcap, Cyrus had been always on the move. His wife, Edna, Rose's mother's sister, had died when he was still young enough to think seriously about re-marrying but a Pullman porter's schedule didn't allow time to remain in one spot long enough to get to know another woman as well as he had known Edna.

The few days he'd had for lay-over were usually spent in small, heavily curtained rooms clogged with card sharps and three-day-old cigar smoke, where bad tasting bathtub gin flowed as long as the money lasted and where a man left just in time to hop his next train out.

He had had the bad luck to earn a Master's degree the same year Herbert Hoover took a twenty percent cut in salary and soup kitchen lines lengthened by the day.

One hour after graduation, he had left Washington and headed to North Carolina on the promise of a teaching position.

When he arrived at the small town, he walked the last two miles to the college. "Take the road straight," the stationmaster said, "-and you can't miss it."

There was no transportation, no people, and the small lean-to houses, horseless wagons, and abandoned wells had taken on the same pockmarked, monochromatic cast left by the blinding dust storms that had rolled in from The Plains.

Leafless trees lined the road leading to the school and the sound of his footsteps was lost in the shifting dust.

No one answered his knock. The door knob came off in his hand. He stepped away and gazed up at the portico to make certain he was at the right place. The school's name was nearly obliterated by the abrasive power of the storm but he could make it out.

He walked around to another, smaller building but those windows were also sand-scarred and he could see nothing inside.

"Someone has to be here. There has to be someone."

The wind carried the parched tone of his voice and brought it back, startling him.

Then: "Professor Greene?"

Cyrus turned, surprised and grateful to hear another human sound. "Yes, I'm Cyrus Greene."

The figure moved toward him, thin and tall and almost blending into the gray surroundings. He drew near and Cyrus recognized him from the picture he had seen in the college newsletter. His face appeared thinner now but his mouth was broad, his nose sharp and his hair close cropped. His eyes were set deep and his brown skin was coated with gray. Cyrus wondered when the man had last tasted a full cup of water. But he appeared sturdy despite his thin build.

"I'm Professor Johnson," he said, extending his hand. "I regret having you come all this distance to be disappointed but there was no way to notify you of these circumstances.

"As you see, the school is closed. Right now, I am the only one here," he said. "Ah, but you must be tired and a bit thirsty. Pardon me. Come this way."

Cyrus followed him to another building, small and windowless and constructed of stone. Inside was dark and the walls felt cool to the touch.

Professor Johnson lit a lantern and the wavering light illuminated several water crocks on the floor near the walls.

"These are nearly empty, but someone will be along in a week or so to refill them." He paused before continuing.

"You know, we have endured a lot, but this is the worst I've seen in my lifetime. Our main building is badly damaged, the livestock have died, and for miles, there is not a blade of grass."

"How long has it been like this?" asked Cyrus, gazing around. The room reminded him of a monk's cell, bare except for the crocks, a table and two straight-back chairs fashioned of rough hewn oak.

"Dust storms are unpredictable. They come up out of nowhere. I saw the sun three times in the last three months."

Cyrus looked at him and saw the gray cast of his skin but saw also that he had not given up the habit of brushing his jacket and trousers.

"But why do you stay?"

Professor Johnson did not answer immediately and Cyrus wondered if he had heard the question. He remained silent and watched the older man carefully pour two cups of water, then unfold a small square of oilcloth and cut two pieces of cornbread from a hard loaf.

"Here we are, Professor Greene. Our daily bread."

Cyrus chewed slowly and ignored the moldy taste, concentrating instead on the sweet water.

"The sun is very important to us," Professor Johnson continued. "Important to man. To all humankind." He spoke as if part of the answer to Cyrus's question had been conveyed in an earlier lecture and he needed only to clarify a minor, but very important point.

"Imagine not seeing the sun for three months, Professor Greene. Some people have been driven mad for lack of light."

He took another sip from his cup and gazed at Cyrus in the dim light. "How long do you estimate the travel time of a slave ship, say, from Goree to Barbados. Or from Elmina in Ghana to the auction block in Charleston?"

He did not wait for an answer but said, "under the best conditions – and I use that term advisedly- under the best circumstances – favorable wind, fast current, no storms, sick cargo overboard with a minimum of delay – it took three months." .

He held up his hand and three fingers cast a shadow on the stone wall. "Three months," he said again. "Ninety days and nights in a reeking hold crammed with a cargo shrieking in a hundred different frightened tongues. And if there had been a whisper, even a hint of rebellion, the hatch remained closed for the entire voyage, except to throw down the buckets of swill.

"Then, as the clipper neared port, the captives were paraded on deck to be washed with sea water and oiled to conceal the wounds.

"Imagine. The sound of that hatch opening. The rush of air, and the blinding, disorienting, sensation of seeing the sun after all those months of darkness. Close your eyes and imagine.

"In difficult times, I sit here in this darkness to commune with the man who built this place, a captive from Mali named Senefe. He was a silversmith who managed to purchase his freedom.

"He built this house and eventually bought the land around it. Bit by bit. Two hundred acres. But he continued to live in this one airless room.

"We bought the land from Senefe's grandson. Every building-the classrooms, dormitories, main house, stables, barns - we constructed in such a way that everything radiates from this point. Like spokes on a wheel. No matter where we are on these grounds, we are able to look at this small place and draw strength from the spirit within this room."

Professor Johnson rose from his chair and seemed to fill the room, nearly blotting out the already dim light. He remained perfectly still and Cyrus wondered if he was listening in the silence to the hollow scrape of the hatch slammed shut, the peg driven in place, and an echoing, angry chorus of unnumbered millions rising against the swell of a wave.

He took his seat again and faced Cyrus. "You said in your letter that you were prepared to teach history." His voice had changed and he spoke rapidly, catching Cyrus further off guard.

"-Well, yes sir, I am."

"Well now, what do you know of Elmina?"

"Elmina?"

"Yes. The infamous fort built by the European slave traders in Ghana. How large were the cells? How thick were the walls? How long were the captives held before the ships were filled and how many females were raped and made pregnant by their jailers?"

Cyrus was astounded. In this dark and cramped space, a whole world had opened before him.

"-And did you know, Professor Greene, that once the captives arrived here, rebellions occurred each and every day? Not just the celebrated ones of Vesey and Turner and Cinque, but widespread revolts, murders of plantation owners, poisoning of their children, fields set afire. These things occurred daily. They are recorded in letters and diaries of the plantation owners themselves but could not be published as general news because the white population would have panicked."

Cyrus took a deep breath. The questions had come at him like bullets, tearing holes in his scholarly shield.

"Well, sir, I – well, no indeed-."

The professor nodded. "Listen, I don't expect you to know these things. Not yet anyway. The point is, you were taught history –'his-story'. Now you should prepare to teach the truth.

" Before coming here, I spent most of my time in a library in Harlem where rare and interesting books tell a different story. When we meet again, we will discuss these stories."

Cyrus wished he did not have to leave. This was where he should be, wanted to be, for the rest of his life. And it was as if the older man read his thoughts.

"Our situation is only temporary. We expect the hatch to slide open very soon. If you are still available, we would enjoy having you join us."

On the way to the depot, Cyrus watched the sun slip through the gray to hang like a sliver of red paint. It cast a brief stab of light and then disappeared, leaving Cyrus alone on the road. The linen handkerchief he had tied across his face blew away and, despite the small sips of water from the bottle he had been given, he felt his tongue crowd the roof of his mouth. He did not rub his eyes for fear of tearing his papery lids.

*** ***

At the station in Washington, he remained on the train. The redcaps had whispered to him that a Bonus Army, 9,000 unemployed war veterans, had invaded the Capitol and the lean-to shacks that had stretched across the Southern landscape now littered the manicured lawns and tree-shaded streets near the White House.

They further warned that tanks had been brought in, and regiments of saber-swinging calvery under the command of a young general named McArthur had galloped down the wide boulevards scattering everything in their path.

A few passengers left the train but Cyrus remained seated, holding his breath against the acrid residue of tear gas.

In New York, he was warned to avoid the flight paths of ruined stockbrokers who shut their eyes and stepped into space fifteen stories up.

He met former classmates with new medical degrees, behind the wheels of taxis, jockeying for fares. He returned to Pennsylvania Station and jostled with five hundred other men waiting to apply for the few available jobs as red caps.

When his name was called, he had thirty seven cents remaining in his pocket.

*** ***

Years later, when the hatch finally slid open as Professor Johnson had predicted, Cyrus could not leave the city. His Pullman days were behind him and he had become part of a circle held to attention by the Lenox Avenue Griots. He had met Matthew and strolled with him into the smoky jazz of Minton's Playhouse. He had dined at Rockland Palace where Father Divine's well-fed angels drowned the biscuits in real butter. And he could not imagine life without Savoy Thursdays and Abyssinia Sundays.

He needed a special vocabulary to explain all of this to Professor Johnson.

'I have decided to remain where I am because I believe black girls need to know that they can indeed fly airplanes. They need to know that Bessie Coleman, in 1921, was the first licensed black female pilot and Madame C.J Walker was the first female self made millionaire, of any color.

' Our boys need to know that one of their ancestors, Benjamin Banneker, helped plan the layout of the nation's capitol, and Dr. Daniel Hale Williams performed the first successful open heart surgery. 'The children need to know this when they're young, before the psychic wound closes and the damage is irreversible.

'But such facts are nowhere to be found in the text books. I was engaged in a running battle with the bureaucracy and finally fired for not adhering to the curriculum. My lawsuit is pending and I intend to win. I'm selling insurance in the interim and will certainly keep you apprised. That small library is everything you described and much more. I am forever grateful to you.'

What Cyrus could not say was that when he stepped from this oasis of rare books, other things unplanned and unforeseen had surged and bumped against him. He could not describe how he had been caught up in the large sounds of Fats Waller's stride piano, payday laughter, bar fights, down-low, brokenhearted blues, and Sunday morning soul-baring backyard spirituals.

So he simply added: "there are other reasons why I cannot leave Harlem."

"Take your time," Professor Johnson replied in his elegant handwriting. Be patient. Enjoy each discovery."

And a year later, his niece had written to him in her precise, schoolgirl handwriting: "Mrs. Burwell, the choir leader, says I have a voice, Uncle Cyrus, but I want to sing something different."

And he had sent her the ticket.

"I'll look after Rose," he promised his late wife's sister.

"I'll look after her."

*** ***

Cyrus had stopped pacing and now stared out of the window, narrowing his eyes against the slanting rays of the afternoon sun flashing off the buildings across 8th Avenue. Those windows that did not have their awnings extended reflected an orange light in the panes, as if fire was consuming the rooms inside.

"I should have looked after her. Paid more attention.."

"What?"

"Nothing, Matthew. Nothing."

Cyrus picked up the ice bucket and headed for the kitchen. He noticed he was sweating, something he never did- not even in the old days when the most difficult passenger challenged him to grin for a nickel tip. Or that time between runs, in that smoky room, when he had held two kings and three aces under his chin and was expected to fold when Big Benny placed his loaded Smith and Wesson on the table. The room had gone quiet and a few players eased toward the door. Even the music slowed, but he hadn't sweated then either. Hadn't thought about it because he was right and there really was nothing to think about.

*** ***

He returned to the living room to find Matthew standing at the window.

"Look."

Cyrus followed his gaze. Rhino stood at the corner. The traffic light blinked red, green, and red again and he waited as if he couldn't decide what to do or which way to go. Suddenly, he glided out, threading through blaring horns and squealing tires. He was slow and casual and

Cyrus wondered if the pink tinted glasses Rhino wore had any effect on his vision.

Cyrus shook his head. "Well, I'll be damned. It's him all right. Why the hell did he have to come back here?"

"I wonder if Babe's seen him yet," Matthew said.

Cyrus turned from the window, placed the bourbon and the ice on a tray and moved toward the door. "I don't know about Babe but we need to talk to Rose."

Matthew picked up his glass and followed.

*** ***

Rhino

...Somebody said the Bronx...

One day, long ago, he had gotten hold of a map and tried to trace the maze of train lines, dotted bus lines criss-crossing streets with numbers, names, places with names, avenues with numbers and dead ends, and more bus lines, but it was confusing. It was easier to walk across the Macombs Bridge at 155th street and take his chances. See where it would lead. All he had to do, as usual, was duck the truant officer.

He turned back at 161st Street after circling in the shadow of the huge courthouse and after two policemen, who first had asked gently if he was lost...then seeing that he actually wasn't white, had threatened to ...beat his no-color black ass back to Harlem where he belonged.

He ran past the Yankee Stadium.

On the bridge, he thought his heart would explode. He lay his head on the railing to catch his breath, waiting for the pain in his chest to go away but the metal was so hot, he thought he had been branded.

He squeezed his eyes shut to fight the tears he knew would come. He was already branded. The policemen told him so.

He looked behind him. They had not followed so he took more minutes to catch his breath.

He leaned over and watched a tug guide a line of coal-filled barges through the murky water. They moved slow and straight and he shaded his eyes wondering where they had come from and where they were going. He watched and waited and gave up after the tenth barge. He wanted to turn away, yet he waited.

...Somebody. Somebody said my mama was in a church in the Bronx...

And he waited.

Chapter Seven

APT. 4A

Rose looked from one to the other, and then turned to stare out of the window. "He can't be! He's actually back in this house?"

"Looks that way," Matthew said. "Of course, his grandmother is still here, so-"

"No," Rose whispered. She leaned back in the chair and began to fan herself with a folded newspaper.

Cyrus touched her shoulder. "Rose, listen. Don't get upset now. Don't- "

She could not answer. When she opened her mouth, the sounds were small and shallow and Matthew thought she was choking. He reached for the ice bucket but the cubes had already begun to melt and so he dipped his handkerchief into the water and spread the cloth, dripping, across her face.

"Wait a minute," Cyrus whispered. "I'll get you a headache powder."

Matthew remained near her, wondering what else he could do. Beyond his role as the bearer of bad news, Rose seemed oblivious of his presence. She ignored him and he watched the water trickle down the side of her face. He heard Cyrus in the bathroom, pulling small things out the cabinet and heard him curse under his breath when he could not find what he was searching for.

Rose removed the handkerchief, looked around, and called out." Cyrus?"

Her voice was shaky with panic and he came running. "Here, take some of this." He filled a glass with water as she placed the powder on her tongue.

"I'm all right now. Just felt dizzy all of a sudden. Must be the heat."

He looked closer. "Listen, Rose, let's – "

"No. No." She rose awkwardly from the chair. "All I need is to lay down a minute. Clear my head..."

"But, Rose," Matthew finally spoke. "Maybe you should – "

"Please! Right now I need to be quiet. Be by myself for a few minutes. When I think things out, I'll come and knock on your door. I will. But right now, I.. oh, God – "

The two men exchanged glances but said nothing. Then Cyrus walked to the door. His apartment was directly across the hall so he did not argue.

"Okay. Okay. We're going to speak to a few more people about this. You lay down. We'll come back later."

He was always awestruck and not a little intimidated by the resemblance Rose bore to his wife; the velvet skin and slightly surprised expression as if she'd just been presented with an unexpected gift.

... God, I wish Edna were here now. Sometimes a woman can speak her mind better than...no, that's not true. I'm avoiding this. Rationalizing as usual.

"We'll be back, Rose. And don't worry. We'll take care of this situation."

*** ***

Rose locked the door and walked unsteadily to her bedroom. She thought of taking a drink, to calm her nerves, but decided against it. She needed to concentrate and try to understand what was happening . She slipped her shoes off and lay on the bed. In the heat, the satin coverlet felt cool against her skin. She took a deep breath and drew in the faint scent of the dusting powder Tommy had given her and which she used only sparingly now.

The first time she saw him, she had been sipping a brandy in the Peacock Bar. He had walked in with a pretty woman on his arm, but she knew he would eventually look in her direction – the way most men did. Someone pressed the jukebox and she hummed along with the deep bass of Jimmy Ricks and the Ravens.

A minute later, the bartender placed a flute of Dom Perignon before her.

"Tommy sends his compliments," he whispered.

Rose did not turn around. In the mirror, she saw that Tommy's companion sat at the table with her back to the bar. Rose leaned to the side and the mirror's beveled edge fractured Tommy's image into infinity. Dark face. Deep set eyes. Cigarette between the teeth when he lit it.

She listened to the music without hearing. Another glass of champagne and Tommy was standing beside her. Up close, she saw that he was even more good looking. His skin resembled silky cinnamon and the slight dimple in his chin disappeared when he smiled. "I heard you sing in The Alley the other night," he whispered. "You sound like that all the time?"

Rose looked at him in the mirror. "Depends."

"On what?"

She raised her glass and the champagne tickled her nose. She wanted to sneeze but instead she held her head back, eyes half closed. "Not on what," she murmured, smiling, "but on whom."

Two nights later, the slat gave way under her bed as they made love and the mattress had fallen to the floor.

"Baby...baby. Look what you make a man do.."

His breath was wet against the nape of her neck and he never missed a beat.

Rose's chest tightened at the memory.

...The times we had. Oh Tommy, baby. What times, what times we had. Thought it was gonna last forever. Like in the movies.

She sat up now and moved away from the coverlet. She did not want her tears to stain it.

She remembered the following week, how surprised she had felt to find him waiting for her outside the blouse factory at quitting time.

She was excited and wanted the other girls to see what a handsome man she had; tall, dark, with the lean muscularity and toe tipping step of a professional boxer. She felt so proud, she could have cried.

"Thought we'd go for a stroll," he said.

"Where?"

"I don't know. Maybe across town," he whispered, taking her arm and heading toward Fifth Avenue, a street she had never walked on during her two years in the city.

... And we had walked by all those big stores, watched the rich folks going in and out. Bonwit Teller. Best and Company. B. Altman. Places I had only read about or seen in the movies. Finally, he walked me into Sloane's, the fanciest furniture place in the world where even the air smelled rich. And that dried up old salesman staring like he ain't never seen colored folks before. Didn't even want to come near us when Tommy asked to see the best bedroom set in the place. Instead, he stared me down...didn't even blink an eye.

And the other customers had stared also, making her aware of the thin cotton dress, good enough for a day's work but a bit tight around the curves.

Her scuffed wedgies, covered with scattered bits of lint, were no longer comfortable, and the scarf that protected her curls from the heat and dust of the power machines suddenly felt too heavy.

In this landscape of fine, light, and precious things, she felt foreign and something inside her shriveled like old bacon.

Tommy glanced at her and went on the offensive with a smile, tapping the salesman on his arm.

"You gonna stand here all day or you gonna show the lady what we asked for?" he said pleasantly.

And Rose had never seen so much cash in her life.

She felt like a queen when Tommy said," give the man your address, sweetheart. This stuff will be in your place by Saturday."

He turned to the salesman for confirmation and they were bathed with whispered, 'good, sirs'. The salesman said 'm'am' and the door was held open as they left.

The taxi cruised through Central Park and Rose gazed at the lake at 110th Street. The water shimmered blue green in the afternoon sun and the trees were thick with birds. Tommy touched her hand. "You're so quiet. What're you thinking?"

"I'm trying not to think about anything right now," she said. "I just want to remember all of this…"

She turned from the window to face him. "This might sound silly, but I wish you could take a picture of my feelings."

"Listen," Tommy whispered. He gathered her in his arms and tilted her chin. "Listen to me, Rose. That voice, we gonna do something with it. It's gonna move you out of the Alley and out of that factory into somewhere you ain't never been before.

"I see how the crowd gets when you open your mouth. You're tellin' them something they need to hear. And feel. God knows I'm feelin' it. You should be singin' regular, not just on weekends. And I bet Blue ain't paying you peanuts."

Rose did not answer. Mrs. Burwell, the choir leader back home had said she had a voice and that she should do something with it. But once she arrived in New York, the place had seemed large and crowded, and in the crowd she heard other voices sounding so much better so she had pushed the idea out of her mind. She had entered that contest in the Alley only because Cyrus persuaded her, wanting to hear what she could do. Beyond the usual prize bottle of nameless sparkling wine she no longer drank after she'd tasted real champagne at the Peacock, she had expected nothing from Blue.

She would have been content to sing all night just to hear the applause and the crowd shout her name each time she finished a number.

She listened now, surprised at what she was hearing.

"I got some plans," Tommy said. "It's gonna be..you and me."

They drove past 125th street and the marquee of the Apollo blazed with Sarah Vaughn's name.

"You gonna get there too, Rose. And that's just one of your stops. First, we gonna start you in the Peacock. Build up a crowd for you. We gonna open up that backroom, put up a small stage."

"In the Peacock?"

"Yeah. The Peacock. You surprised?"

"I'm confused."

"Well, don't be."

He leaned away from her, rested his head on the back of the seat, and gazed at the ceiling. "I'm gonna teach you to look beyond smoke and mirrors, Rose. Sometimes, folks are more than they seem to be. Truth is, you looking at one of the silent partners."

She said nothing, not knowing what a silent partner was.

But Tommy was going to help her become a real singer, a star just like Billie Holiday. And most of all, she and Tommy were going to be together. Together.

"Now listen," he took a small notepad from his jacket and began to make notes. "We're gonna change the lights so we can play up your pretty face… and we're gonna – "

…And that was the way it was supposed to be.

Now she stood near the window and pulled the curtains apart allowing sunlight to filter through half opened blinds. Tommy had never officially moved in but had had her apartment decorated with the new furniture, the mauve satin quilts and pillows; her favorite chaise lounge was covered in rich pink damask and everywhere were varying shade of pink, beige and coral.

"These colors," he had said one night as he lay next to her, "look real good against you."

By transforming her surroundings, he had put his stamp, his seal, in place, letting her know that her earlier affairs, if there were any, were over. He was now the one in her life despite his relationship with Babe.

She asked only once about Babe, the woman she had seen in the Peacock and who ran the numbers operation around on the avenue.

" – She's my business partner…"

-In a tone crisp and quiet which meant Babe was more than business but Rose never asked again. She felt that he would eventually leave Babe. It was only a matter of time.

On another occasion, he had said, "if it's good for you and good to you, well that's fine. But shake it loose if it's not. You don't need nobody ain't gonna be a help to you. You can do bad by yourself."

Shake it loose. Never. I loved him better than she ever did. We were gonna last forever. Now he's gone. And Rhino is back.

She had been pacing the floor and stopped suddenly. "Why didn't Tommy kill him when he had that chance?"

The dizziness came again and she lay on the chaise, glad to be alone. No one, not even Cyrus knew how or why it had really happened. She turned over and heard Rhino's voice echo in her head, the raspy sound of his voice as clear as if he had confronted her yesterday.

*** ***

That day, they had been alone in the hallway, yet he looked over his shoulder like a conspirator.

"What I seen could stay in my cap," he said. "You know, between you and me."

His face was inches away from her, his mouth parted, and his expression was as close to a smile as he could manage.

"Babe don't have to know," he whispered.

And she had stared at him, unable to speak.

What Rhino had seen the night before, from his grandmother's bathroom window was Tommy, naked, in Rose's kitchen. Tommy opening the refrigerator – the stark light illuminating his muscular frame as he pulled a bottle of champagne from the shelf, and the door snapping shut to bathe him in darkness again.

And moments later, Rose's laughter, heavy with excitement, had flowed through the courtyard and washed over Rhino like a wave.

He wondered what she was doing and how she was doing it. Was she lying back, legs apart, moving, rolling, tangled in her damp sheets.

He squeezed his eyes closed and leaned against the basin with his pants around his ankles. Suddenly he called her name, held his breath, then sank to his knees and pressed his face against the wet wall.

*** ***

The following day, when Rose came up the stairs, he had eased from behind the dumbwaiter enclosure.

"How you doin?"

Rose stopped. "You never asked before how I was doing. Why you want to know now?"

"Cause –" "he hesitated, gazing at her. "Maybe – "

"Maybe what?? Come on, Rhino. I got no time for your foolishness!"

"Oh no?" He had stepped nearer. "Got no time for me but you got time for Babe's man, is that it?"

Rose, about to turn away, stood still. "Listen, Rhino. Tommy is my manager. I'll be singing steady and he's arranging things."

She felt the anger rising in her. Why was she explaining anything to him. She never even spoke to him.

"And what else is he arrangin'?"

"What are you talkin' about?"

"I'm talkin' about what I seen last night, that's what. Next time you got somebody strollin' the stroll in your kitchen who ain't supposed to be there, let 'im pull on his drawers or else pull on your shades, either one."

Rose started toward him. "You damn, nosey son of a bitch. You keep out of my business, you hear?"

"I hear you." He turned to go. "But like I said, this could stay in my cap, but now Babe gonna hear also unless –"

"Unless.." He turned on the steps. Rose smelled the soured sweat and backed away.

"Rhino. What. Do. You. Want?"

He stared at her, confronted with a question he could not answer. He looked at the velvet skin and slightly slanted eyes, the round mouth glossy with lipstick he had dreamed of tasting on all the nights he could not sleep and had kept watch at his bathroom window. He stared, mesmerized by the shimmering lights refracted in the small diamonds in her ear lobes.

"What. Do. You. Want?" came to him again, this time from far away. He strained to answer but his head began to hurt and the pain crowded out intelligent response. All he could think of was velvet.

If he could only make her understand that all he wanted was to fold himself in the dark warmth of her. To hear her voice call his name. He wanted to breathe her in, like the scent of a forgotten perfume.

...What. Do.You.Want.? came at him like an echo from the depth of a cave.

What. Do.. came out of a fog, causing his head to spin.

...Why couldn't he just drink her in. Like water. Then she and the velvet would become a part of him and he would no longer have to-

"What do you want, Rhino?"

"I don't. I don't..." He held out his hand and Rose shrank against the wall.

Don't you touch me!"

He was surprised at the horror in her voice. His eyes narrowed and his voice dropped again.

"Aah, Rose. You don't have to do nuthin'. Nuthin', you hear. Just lemme-"

His mind went blank. Plans, schemes, and all the unfocused anger and longing that had sustained him like so much scaffolding, collapsed and fell away. He sank to his knees and pressed his mouth against her thigh.

She slapped him hard, knocking off his glasses.

"Don't you touch me! Don't touch me!"

He fumbled for his glasses and stood up. "Rose. Rose. Please..."

The sound of his weakness, high and hopeless, made her angrier. "Listen, Rhino. Anything you got on your mind, you clear it with Tommy. Go ahead. Ask him if you can touch me. Otherwise you can keep on dreamin', and dreamin ain't gonna make it happen!"

She turned away and he stared, trying to hold on to the one chance that was slipping away. She was moving beyond his grasp, disappearing like everything else and leaving in its wake the broken, familiar fragments of dreams.

The anger rose in his chest again, tight, threatening to cut his breath off.

"Like I said, this ain't gonna stay in my cap. We gonna see what Babe'll do about this."

"Go on and tell her. See if I care."

"You gonna care when she come at you with her ten cent pistol."

Rose tried not to look at him but she knew that what he said was true. Babe was a Charleston woman with a fast hand and a hard reputation.

...A ten cent pistol. A can of lye. I'm not ready to have no can of lye thrown in my face.

She put her hand to her hip. "Who's gonna believe you? A four eyed worm who couldn't see straight if your life depended on it. Who's gonna believe you?"

"Babe will, that's who..! "

"Listen, if that woman comes after me, my uncle's comin' after you."

"Don't drag Cyrus into this. He wasn't the one all in between Tommy's legs. You was."

Rose watched him watch her. His pupils seemed to dance out of control. She wanted to push his face into the wall.

Finally, she turned and walked quickly up the stairs, feeling the weight of his eyes crawling up her back.

At the top of the landing, she leaned over the banister. "I'm tellin' you, Rhino, if you was the last man on the planet, I wouldn't even let you smell it!"

There was no answer but she knew he was still there. She entered the apartment quickly, double locked the door, and reached for the phone.

*** ***

Tommy had been alone in the candy store when Rhino strolled in and stood near the entrance. He scanned the small space, then moved further inside. He was not interested in the racks of magazines, the shelves of candy and gum, or the jars of loose, two-for-a-penny cigarettes that crowded the counter. He was looking for Babe.

Without a word, Tommy reached over the counter and grabbed him by the collar. "Listen, man. I know why you here and I'm givin' your sorry ass five seconds to clear the door."

Rhino's fingers curled around the knife in his back pocket but when he brought it out, Tommy twisted it out his hand.

"Now look here. C'mon, lemme show you how to work this."

Before Rhino could answer, Tommy spun him like a top and held the blade to his neck, not deep enough to kill him but hard enough to send him howling out the door.

At Harlem Hospital, an expert in cutlery marveled that the trachea and major veins were still intact. Nevertheless, he had to embroider Rhino's neck with one hundred stitches and Tommy's artwork became the talk of 8th Avenue.

"Man, you see that tattoo?"

"What that fool do to get that?

"Heard he jumped bad, tried to sell wolf tickets to Tommy, of all people."

"You mean Tommy? Big bad six feet four Tommy? Shit. Damn sure IS a fool."

"But they don't call him Rhino for nuthin'. Cat got some tough hide, man."

" –And ugly to boot!"

"He's too mean to croak, is what I say. If it had been anybody else, their head woulda been clean off, but his wasn't even hangin' sideways. Rhino is one mean mamma jamma."

"And ugly to boot!"

Fourteen days after he had been sliced, stitched, and sent home, Rhino lingered in the Peacock nursing a gin through a straw and watching through the window as the numbers players moved in and out of the candy store across the avenue.

Three hours after the last figure, the final payoff was made. He waited a minute longer, then left the bar and strolled through the traffic, slow and deliberate.

At the curb, he moved fast and pushed his way into the store before Babe could lock the door.

Tommy rushed from the back when she shouted but had no time to duck the spray of bullets ricocheting in the small space. Three hit him in the chest and arm and he sprawled back onto the pile of boxes behind the counter. One grazed Babe's neck as she ran screaming out the door into the street. A minute later, the patrol car that pulled up for its nightly take, picked up Rhino instead.

That was the way everyone said it had happened. Babe screaming and running up 8th Avenue like a wild woman with J.R. and Bad-Sam running after her, trying to calm her. And the number spot closing for three days until Babe's sister, Nola, came up from Charleston to take care of the funeral and pay off the weekly players and then stay until things got right again .

There were thirty Cadillacs in the procession, three for the flowers alone. The Blind Allley, Connie's Pool Hall, the numbers joints and several stores closed their doors in observance and those that remained open had black-framed notices posted in the windows.

Bankers and business men, players and pimps came from Boston, Baltimore, Philadelphia, and Atlantic City. The Peacock Bar pulled in an extra cook and re-stocked its shelves in preparation for the marathon wake.

People lined the curbs as the motorcade wound its way up 8th Avenue, stopping traffic. The cars paused to play the doleful chimes under the viaduct near the Polo Grounds where a steady stream of Giants fans had once left their bets with Tommy before going into the game.

From her window, Rose watched the line of chrome and black gleam in the sun as each car made a U turn far up the avenue, and then once more slow to a stop downstairs in front of the candy store. She watched Babe step from her limousine and place a single white carnation at the entrance.

The chimes started again and Rose closed her ears. She concentrated on Tommy's silk bathrobe folded at the foot of the bed. His toothbrush was in the glass on the basin in the bathroom and the splits of champagne were in the refrigerator, waiting.

She closed her eyes, cradled her head in her folded arms and thought about singing.

...Maybe.. if I open my mouth to those soft notes he loves so much, especially when we make love, he will appear, smiling, and let me know that the whole thing – the cars, the chimes, even Babe with the carnation- it's all a mistake. And all those people lining the curb are really waiting for someone else.

*** ***

She switched off the fan on the table. It was only circulating the room's hot air and the hum of the motor, small as it was, irritated her. In the silence she became aware of the ache in her temples.

...My head – feels like it's gonna burst.

Another minute passed before she was able to ease up from the chaise. In the bathroom, she leaned close to the mirror, trying to explore beneath the layer of circles that darkened her eyes. Her face appeared dry and ashen and the deep lipstick had taken on the vivid aspect of stage makeup. She touched the side of her neck and watched a thin vein stir, rolling like a worm beneath the surface of her skin.

I'm gonna have a stroke. A stroke.

The sound of the door bell cut the silence and the face in the mirror blurred as she moved away.

It rang again and she sat on the edge of the bathtub, her hands folded in her lap.

...it's not Cyrus, she thought. And it's not Matthew either.

A light, insistent, tapping began, soft, hypnotic.

She rose from the edge of the tub and her hands fumbled in the medicine cabinet searching among the cold cream, peroxide, and toothpaste and came to rest on Tommy's straight razor.

"-Well."

She leaned against the bathroom door, and then turned toward the dark corridor leading to the source of the noise.

"Well," she whispered again, and moved like a thief.

The tapping grew, and then halted as abruptly as it had begun. She pressed her face against the door and heard the soft padding of someone sliding away.

In one motion, she jerked the door open but the hall was empty except for a lingering odor. It was heavy and sour and reminded her of old clothing.

It was him. I know it was him...

Across the hall, a lock turned and she slipped the razor into her pocket before Cyrus opened his door.

"Rose! I thought you'd be lying down. Is everything all right? You feeling any better?"

"A little." Her hand remained in her pocket, covering the razor.

"Good," he said, frowning slightly. "We were coming to check on you before making the rounds."

...Only doctors made rounds, Rose thought, irritated that Cyrus could sound so formal even in the worst circumstances.

...A murderer is on the loose in the damn house and Cyrus is going on rounds.

She looked at him and wanted to laugh.

"Rounds?" she repeated.

"Yes. We're going to speak to Effie."

The impulse to laugh withered at the mention of Effie's name.

Effie Cummings, Rose thought, wore her widowhood like a neon cross and managed to act as if she were alone whenever they passed each other in the hallway.

...like she's the only woman in the world ever lost a husband. I lost somebody too. Even if I wasn't actually married to him.

"What are you going to see her about? What can she do?"

"We want to make sure she knows about Rhino," Matthew added.

She looked at him, wondering if he had heard the sound that had brought her to the door.

"Then," Cyrus continued, "we're going to talk to the Morgans and to Mrs. Dillard. You want to come?"

Rose shook her head and backed into her apartment. "No. Not yet. Not now."

She locked the door and listened as they moved toward the stairs.

In her bedroom, she laid the razor on the night table where a narrow shaft of sunlight illuminated the pearl handle.

...Well, let him come again.

The thought was like a half-remembered tune she had heard somewhere and now was caught in its rhythm.

"Let him come..."

She looked in the mirror and smoothed her hair away from her forehead. She was still sweating. She held her hair tight and watched the lines fade from above her brows.

...He robbed me. Took away my man. My life. I would give anything, everything, my voice, my soul, to have him back. Nothing else means anything.

She turned from the mirror and studied the pearl handle again.

...Let Rhino step to me and they will carry him away in pieces. I'll slice his ass so thin, Armour Bacon will wonder how I did it.

Chapter Eight

APT 3A

Effie Cummings' living room held a certain, close, comfort: a heavy-armed, tapestry-covered sofa faced two deep cushioned velvet wing chairs. The floors were thick carpeted and soft lighting was made softer by pale silk pleated lamp shades.

The few times Matthew had visited, he'd felt the urge to remove his shoes and stretch out on the sofa or even the carpet where he knew sleep would overtake him in a matter of seconds.

Now he sat in the wing chair and watched her move toward Cyrus to pour him a second cup of coffee. He thought he saw Cyrus hold his breath so that Effie would not detect the odor of bourbon. He also saw him smile as Effie leaned over him.

The silk scarf covering her head inched back each time she moved, revealing her bone white hair. Still, she was elegant and easy going and nothing like he remembered at the time of her husband's death.

Matthew continued to watch her.

...Still won't tint that hair. Can't be no more than forty and seems like she's deliberately trying to make herself look ugly. Her old man's a memory now. Gone. Somebody needs to pull her coat to the fact.

He thought of Sandra and wondered how she would react if he were to die suddenly, then decided that mourning a year or so wasn't all that bad.

"Listen," he said as Effie approached to fill his cup, "we didn't mean to disturb you, for you to go through all this trouble."

Effie waved her hand. "This is no trouble, not at all. What is it you wanted to talk about?"

"Well," Matthew continued, "seems we got a problem on our hands. That boy, Rhino, is back and we need to make sure he hasn't come back to stay. At least not in this house."

Effie returned the coffee pot to the tray. The pot was old silver, heavy with curliques and with a long spout that gleamed in the reflected light and Matthew wondered how much time she spent polishing it.

He watched her re-arrange her cup on the tray and check the sugar cubes. Finally, she cleared her throat. "But his grandmother is right downstairs. She raised him in this house."

She glanced quickly from Matthew to Cyrus. "Don't get me wrong. I'm not defending what he did. God knows, Babe took it hard enough. And I'm not arguing his right to live here, I'm saying how can you keep him out?"

"After what he did," Matthew said, "I'm not sure he has the *right* to live here. He's dangerous."

"Besides," Cyrus added, "I have an idea he might come after Rose."

The silence lasted half a minute as Effie turned and gazed at him steadily.

"Why do you say that? Your niece never impressed me as being afraid of any man."

Matthew studied the design on the coffee pot, waiting for Cyrus to respond.

"Well," Cyrus stammered. He did not want his private suspicions to become public knowledge. Not yet, anyway. "Well, you know- she's a woman alone," he answered lamely.

"So am I," Effie replied matter of factly, "and I'm not expecting him to bother me. Would you like more cream?"

Her voice trailed in her wake as she left the room.

In the kitchen, she opened the refrigerator, leaned down and breathed in the vaporous air, hoping to damp down the sudden anger.

...Rose is afraid of Rhino. Afraid. That woman with her parade of men. Changed them faster than she changed her stockings. How can she be afraid of Rhino?

She lifted the cold milk bottle and held it against her face. Her breathing was not as easy as it should have been and there was that tightness in her chest again.

...Now the chickens have come home to roost. All those nights I lay awake and listened to that whore's creaking bed, and all that groaning. And her loud singing in the morning after, like she was just so happy. She performed extra hard when the windows were open. Put on a show for the whole neighborhood. Sometimes it got so bad, the pictures on my walls shook. And the night her cheap bed finally broke, I thought for sure she was going to fall through my ceiling.

And Matthew thinks Rhino is the dangerous one.

The feeling intensified and she leaned against the door of the refrigerator , praying it would pass quickly.

...Don't get too worked up, the doctor said. Nothing's worth it.

...But sometimes, sometimes, the feeling just comes out of nowhere. Like a loose brick from a rooftop. Imagine. Rose with that army of men. And me -with the only one I ever had. Or thought I had..

She reached for the can of evaporated milk and slammed the door of the refrigerator. A tray fell from a shelf inside.

"Effie," Cyrus called. "You all right?"

She did not answer but returned to the living room with the creamer and sat down opposite the two men. Matthew had been humming a soft tune she thought she recognized but he had stopped abruptly-in mid-note it seemed- when she came in.

She tried to look beyond the nonchalance and speculate if something-some small coded gesture that spoke of her condition –had passed between the two men in her absence.

She reached for her cup. The coffee had cooled but she drank it anyway because her hands needed a weight between the fingers to keep them from shaking.

Well Rhino and the chickens have come home together. What do you know. Now let's see if that faded floozie gives him the same evil look she gives me every time we pass in the hallway.

Finally, to break the silence, she said. "I don't know if Rhino should move. I really don't. Seems to me that whatever happened, happened. It's in the past. Perhaps we should all try to live and let live."

She raised her cup to her mouth and ignored the look that passed between the two men.

An hour later, Effie closed the door and leaned against it, feeling the small trickle of sweat run down her arms. The scent of Cyrus's cologne lingered in the air along with the faint, not unpleasant, odor of bourbon.

When he had passed her on the way out, she wanted to pull at his sleeve and explain that what she had said was not what she meant. Rhino was indeed dangerous, always had been but as far as she was concerned, Rose, in her own brazen way, was just as bad.

She returned to the living room and collected the cups and saucers, conscious of the small, thin sound they made when she placed them on the tray.

The silence around her was also different, more like a ballroom after the last dancers had gone out into the night, leaving only shadows and memories to keep her company.

Now Matthew's tune came to her in its suggestive echo:

... To spend one night with you
In our own rendezvous
That's my desire.

...Why couldn't Cyrus, at least, have stayed a little longer. We could have talked.

She closed her eyes.

But how do you tell a man that his niece's skin was too beautiful to describe. How do you tell him that the woman should not walk down the street in those tight print dresses and those high heels that caused cars to squeal to a stop.

...I saw how she'd look at a man, carelessly, as if she didn't give a damn whether he smiled or not. And most men would be grinning from ear to ear. I heard that when she walks into the Peacock or the Blind Alley, the men fall all over themselves to buy her a drink.

Effie moved toward the kitchen with the tray, disturbed by the wild, fast rhythm in her chest and trying to remember the last time a man had greeted her, even casually.

...So Rhino was after Rose and Tommy had to die because of it.

I should've said something about Tommy coming up and down these steps, bold as brass, and Babe right around the corner, working so hard. Should've spoken to Babe or at least to Cyrus. Instead, I watched and, like everyone else, pretended not to see.

She was standing in front of the sink, staring at the broken cup in her hand and the pieces that lay near the drain.

I didn't say a word. But isn't that what happened to me?

Everyone knowing what had been going on and no one, not one soul, saying a word.

The air seemed to leave the room. Effie sat near the window and reached for the small paper fan wedged between the sugar container and the flour jar on the counter.

The fan, shaped like a heart on a popsicle stick, was inscribed 'Holy Deliverance Center of Light' on one side. The reverse had a picture of the singing, hand-clapping, red robed choir.

Above their heads, in bold letters, a caption read 'Peace and Love'.

The salty and familiar taste of blood covered her tongue and Effie realized she had bitten the inside of her mouth again.

Peace and love.

She gazed at the fan, not wanting to think about it but the stifling odor of flowers and the melancholy strains of organ music slipped through the thin membrane of forgetfulness.

And again, she heard the phrase slide from the mouth of the Reverend Benjamin Braithwaite:

Peace and love.

She saw now, in her mind's eye, that the main meeting room of the Holy deliverance Center of Light had been much too small for her husband's funeral. Maxwell had, after all, died of a heart attack; he had not been killed in an accident. Or murdered. Yet extra chairs had been set up as more and more mourners arrived. She watched them waver like shadows in the dim light and wondered if her husband had actually known all these people.

She saw the Deliverance paper fans whirl, out of sync, like a flight of disoriented birds.

But some fans held steady, pressed against tight mouths, smothering sounds she could not, at the time, quite fathom.

The odor of the red and yellow roses, gaudy in its abundance, nauseated her. A thicket of gardenias, gladiolas, and day lilies overflowed the casket and seemed to draw what little air there was out of the room.

The heat had given a sharp edge to the mix of perfume, aftershave, and apprehension, yet some fans remained motionless, waiting.

"Peace and love," the reverend murmured, pausing in his nervous eulogy. "Brother Maxwell has gone on now and left this sorrowful woman to mourn."

Sorrowful. Effie had sat, rigid, on the edge of the wooden folding chair, trying hard to draw inward.

She would never have considered joining this church, had done so only to please Maxwell who had always seemed vaguely dissatisfied with everything she did.

"This sorrowful woman," Reverend Braithwaite repeated slamming the high pulpit. Effie leaned forward, raising her veiled face to look for meaning in the reverend's recessed, searching eyes, and he had whispered "to my sister in sorrow" his arms stretched wide in supplication.

Effie thought it was natural, though a bit theatrical, for the reverend to go down on his knees in front of Maxwell's casket, in front of the head-shaking congregation crammed shoulder to shoulder that hot July day.

She had studied the sweating faces in the gathering. Her husband had only been a deacon. She could not imagine such a large turnout if the reverend himself had died.

She was not involved in the affairs of the church and she did not know.

But Hazel Harper Braithwaite, the reverend's wife, had known, months ago, and had gone crying to Deacon Simon.

"He talks in his sleep," she whispered tearfully, "and guess what he said..."

Deacon Simon touched the tips of his arthritic fingers together in prayerful attitude and advised her to keep quiet. Trust him. He would get to the bottom of everything.

And he ran to spread the news as fast as big feet and bad legs could move.

Effie remembered the church dining hall after the funeral, crowded with food and more flowers. The fans were gone, allowing her to stare into the masks of strangers.

Then Hazel Braithwaite appeared, gently touching at her arm, deftly guiding her through the floral tributes, away from the crowd, and four steps down into the small, single-booth bathroom where she carefully locked the door.

They faced each other in the crowded space and Hazel, without preliminary, whispered, "you ain't no widow 'cause you ain't never been no wife, you bitch!"

–shocking Effie so that she stumbled back against the wall.

"What's wrong with you, Hazel. Have you gone crazy?"

Hazel stepped closer, her usually strong choir-voice never rising above a whisper. "Once I thought so, Effie. It had got so bad I thought I was gonna lose my mind, but now… now everything's all right…"

"What?"

""All that sorrowful shit." Hazel imitated her husband, drawing the sound of the word through her nostrils and expelling it in a rush, as if to get the smell of something bad out of her system. "Sorrowful! Truth is, Effie, you wasn't woman enough to hold on to your man. You was being bullshitted while Maxwell was out scouting."

Effie worked her way through this maze of language.

She understood Hazel's crudeness and her vulgarity because it had always been a part of her, lying just beneath the veneer of desperate gentility. Hazel had always smiled the longest and the widest and had always fanned herself the fastest with that silly, customized, initialed paper fan.

The fan had disappeared with the pretense and Hazel's voice rose. "Maxwell was scouting," she said again, relishing the sound of the word and the look of confusion on Effie's face.

"Scouting," Effie said, trying to understand. "What -?"

"Boy scouting," Hazel said, her voice dropping to a whisper again. "That nasty dog was fucking my husband more than I was. Well, Maxwell's gone. He's dead and I'm glad. You hear me! Damn glad! A heart attack was too good for him."

Effie, speechless, had stared at the door slammed shut, had listened to the quick, neat scrape of Hazel's thin heels on the steps leading to the dining hall and then heard something flutter inside her like the leathery wings of a night creature.

And the sound never coming out because by then, the diamond-shaped wall tiles had started to shimmer around the mirror, and she saw the small wash basin dance.

The ceiling somehow appeared where the floor should have been and the walls trembled and fell away. Pain uncoiled in her chest like a heavy snake, crowding her heart, squeezing until her lungs caught fire.

When she fell to her knees, clawing at the fine black veil pressing against her face, she could only murmur, "Lord, please, please...don't let me die here... not here.."

*** ***

Effie placed the paper fan on the kitchen shelf and leaned back in the chair. The afternoon sky had darkened and a slight breeze ruffled the blinds. A storm was coming with the promise of cool weather but she could not relax.

She fingered the silk scarf, absently tracing the design, and finally pulled it from her head.

No need to glance in the mirror or study the reflection in the window. The hair was still the way it was.

"Shock. Grief. Loss. The funeral was too much for her," the doctors, who didn't know the story, had said.

"Bone white," sighed the parade of visitors, many of whom knew better but offered an opinion anyway. "That hospital done went and turned your poor head bone-white, Effie. If I was you, I"d sue. My sister's brother in law's cousin is a lawyer."

Others said; "Honey, look like your husband tried to take you with him. You hold on, now. Hold on and everything's gonna be all right. Time heals."

Time heals.

A month later, cleaning out Maxwell's desk, Effie found the other insurance policy made out to Reverend Braithwaite. She also found a dozen or so letters. She read only one. That afternoon, she paid a visit to the church.

"I want this money, Benjamin." It was an effort to even look at him.

He sat behind the desk, nodding in studied sympathy. He had a thick athletic build and his shoulders bunched like hams when he rested his elbows on the blotter. His skin was brown and smooth and his eyes were set deep under thin brows.

"Now you know, Effie, Maxwell meant for the church to have this policy.."

"I don't know about the church," Effie said, opening her purse again. "I think he meant for you to have it. It has your name on it."

Reverend Braithwaite fingered the policy as if seeing it for the first time. His eyes widened, and then narrowed as if exposed to a sudden flash of light. "Why, yes. It does."

'Twenty thousand dollars is a lot of money, Reverend."

"Yes. Yes. It certainly is."

"-But I figured you wouldn't be needing it after I started reading some of these letters."

Reverend Braithwaite had been leaning back in his chair gazing at the ceiling, thinking of his windfall and how to end this irritating woman's visit.

Now the chair slammed forward and the glazed politeness disappeared. He stared at the envelopes spread like a deck of cards on the desk between them.

Effie leaned back. "I got at least a dozen more, Reverend."

*** ***

And so it had been done quickly and with no small amount of ceremony though the church had not been nearly as crowded as it had been for Maxwell's funeral.

An impassioned sermon, Braithwaite handing a small plaque and a large check to the bereaved widow as a photographer from the Amsterdam News captured the occasion.

" –Indeed a pleasure to see that the widow of one of our most dedicated parishioners is taken care of. Deacon Cummings left this generous gift to the church, but in recognition of –"

And Effie, stylish in a pink dress and broad brimmed black straw hat that hid her hair, had gazed modestly at the flashing bulbs, then shook hands warmly with Hazel Harper Braithwaite sitting in the front row. Effie had leaned close and wondered if the sound she heard was the grinding of Hazel's teeth behind the customized fan.

*** ***

Effie gazed out over 8th Avenue and watched scattered drops darken the pavement. A streak of lightning bathed the landscape in brilliant relief an instant before the downpour and she could no longer see the sidewalk, only vague shapes running for shelter. The storm shifted and blew a gust in her face, forcing her to close the window.

She listened to the water beat against the glass, as she picked up the scarf again and wrapped it around her head.

...No one really says anything now but I see it in their faces. Their eyes tend to wander, trying to move away from this scarf. They're embarrassed to look because this hair lets them know that I know what no one would tell me. Even Matthew couldn't help staring when he was here and he sees me every day.

She went to the sink to clear away the bits of glass.

...Why did Matthew have to stare so hard? Did he know? Did Cyrus know about Maxwell?

She picked up a large shard of glass and smashed it into the counter.

...Now they want me to help. To help them because Rhino is back and Rose is afraid. To hell with them. To hell with her. She helped herself to someone else's man. Let's see what that little bitch can do now.

Chapter Nine

APT 3B

At 3.a.m. Stanislaw Morgan turned over in bed, bone tired but unable to fall asleep. He lay in the silence for a few minutes thinking of Matthew and Cyrus and their earlier visit and tried to shut his eyes, hold them together tightly and imagine that the visit had been only a dream. But he could not control the feeling rising in his chest, threatening to strangle him. He lay still a moment longer, then finally eased his hand across his wife's shoulder.

"Clo," he whispered, "wake up."

Clothilde opened her eyes instantly, blinked, then sat up.

"What is it, Honey? What's the matter?"

"Listen," he said, propping himself up on a pillow. "I been thinkin' about things."

Clothilde rubbed her eyes, glanced at the clock on the nightstand, then stared at her husband, at his face drawn and dark, his wiry frame, and the map of fatigue grooved around his thin mouth.

"What things? You mean the visit, that's what you mean?"

Stanislaw felt his wife's rapid breathing and nearly changed his mind. Then he said softly, "Yes. If what Matthew and Cyrus say is so, we got a problem. That Rhino man is a criminal, a convict, and he gonna have all kind of police and government people spyin' 'round the place."

"You mean we gotta move??"

"I don't know. Maybe. Lemme think."

He sat up and swung his legs over the edge of the bed. They felt leaden but he ignored the familiar pain and he clasped his hands together.

"Can you imagine a murderer livin' in this house? A murderer?" He shook his head, trying to adjust to the enormity of this new situation. "A murderer," he said again. "You know in Antigua we would have made short work of someone like him. Remember slick Nick who did in old Mr. Charles with that rusty cutlass? No matter that Charles had double-crossed him in a scheme. Court last one day and next dawn, slick Nick drew his last breath. People still talking on it.

"And don't mention Richard, the vegetable thief who used to lay in wait for your crop to come in. Ain't lift one fingernail to plant, but lift plenty hand to steal it. We ain't see judge nor jury. No, sir. Boys 'round the way spring that trap, now they makin' style on one-hand Richie. That's Antigua way. But here now, they give a murderer a two year vacation to regroup his strength so he can come out and do it again. I don't know what kind a system this place got but it ain't safe for Sara. Maybe we ought not to have brought her here in the first place."

The pain in Clothilde's chest nearly made her choke. She reached over him to click on the small lamp on the nightstand. She could not believe what she was hearing and needed to look in his eyes as he spoke. "Stan, what are you saying?"

"I'm saying that maybe she'd be better off back –"

"No! I ain' goin' back, Stan. Not back to that outside wash tub and that spigot with the rusty tastin' water, not back to that bad smellin' oil to heat the water to wash my skin. Every time you look around, is water I was boilin'. You'd a thought I was mid-wifin' or somethin'. No. No. I ain't goin' back."

"I didn't say you. I said her. We could send her back to stay with your sister, Dora."

"How you mean??" Clothilde's voice rose. "How you gonna cut off the calf from the cow. I born her. Where I go, she go. She ain't going back to no rusty water and neither is me!!"

She leaned up on one elbow, her thin lips marking a grim line on her face. Her eyes grew large and she brushed her hair away from her shoulders. She was ready for a fight.

"Clo," Stan said gently, "we got a man here who is a murderer. I see trouble if she stay."

" –And I see trouble if she go," Clothilde said. "I see trouble. Period. You come over on contract to pick grapes for three months. I come to visit for three weeks. Is over a year we here and no papers in sight."

"Hush, woman! Calm your mouth." He tip toed across the room and quickly closed the window. "You want somebody to call us out?" Be quiet!"

He returned to sit on the edge of the bed. He walked slowly and his shoulders were slightly stooped. "That lawyer is workin' on the papers and I'm payin' him what little I can put by every week. But I don't know. Now he says he got to contact somebody big in the court and they need money too. Sometime s I feel like I'm workin' for the lawyer alone."

The room had become too warm and he crossed the floor again to open the window.

"But that's another matter, Clo. Right now, this place ain't so good for the girl. It just ain't safe."

"Then we move," Clothilde whispered. She leaned forward and pressed her hand lightly on his shoulder. "We find somewhere else to live. But I ain't goin' back and neither is Sara.

"I mean, what chance does the girl have back there?" she continued in a softer voice. "The most she can be is somebody's front desk clerk in the white man's hotel. And if he get fresh with her, she out of a job 'cause I gonna have to go break up the place. And you is a peace lovin' man. I know you don't want no scandal to your name."

She put her arms around his shoulders and drew him to her. "Think what it means for her to be here, Stan. She's a smart girl, up for a scholarship. I don't know much about this new law but people say colored children can go to any school now. Any school. She can study and be somethin' more than a maid or a clerk. Would that happen back home?"

Stan did not answer but switched off the light and lay back with his arms folded behind his head. The small room was sparsely furnished with an old iron bed, an unpainted chest and two small night tables. He wished he could do better for his family but other things always seemed to get in the way.

Finally, he turned to her and whispered, "well, it's settled. We movin' as quick as we can put our fingers on the money. I gonna look for more work downtown. Meanhwile, you stick to that girl like a shadow 'till I find out more about this Rhino person. He sounding to me like a real villain."

Clothilde knew there was nothing more to say. She lay in the dark, eyes wide, watching the shadows dance across the ceiling from the lights of passing cars.

Sometimes the lights merged, crossed each other, then went their separate ways. She listened to the rhythm of her husband's soft snoring and was glad he was able to fall asleep. He lay spread eagled, mouth open slightly, with one leg resting on her thigh. His frame was so thin, she felt his chest move with every breath he took.

In the darkened room, she felt the sudden sting of her tears.

...Aah, more trouble now. I shoulda known it when my left eye started to jumpin' ..

She moved his leg gently and pulled a light spread over him. No matter how hot it got, he needed a cover or he'd wake in the morning, sneezing.

"Ah, darlin' how you gonna work two jobs. One is hard enough for you. Besides, I don't want to leave this place just now, noisy and crowded as it is. Effie was my first friend when I came here. And Mr. Paige's music, when it's soft and sweet, always puts my mind at ease.

She thought of the way it was back home and out of the dark, the other memory moved in so quickly, it caught her off guard.

...No. we ain't none a us goin' back 'cause things ain't changed one bit. Time ago, hotel manager promised me a front desk job. No more makin' beds he said. Me, fifteen, and didn't know any better than to listen to the sweet talk. When I find myself in trouble, he gone for home back in Canada. No. I don't need to go back. Trouble there. Trouble here. Is all the same, no matter what.

She checked the covers on her husband, and then rolled over on her side, feeling her rapid heartbeat.

I was lucky. Sweet Dora take me to the old hill woman and Mama never know. And after all my sorrow, I meet this decent man.

She lifted her head and kissed Stan on his shoulder. He tasted faintly of salt.

We can't send this girl back. Pretty as she is, I can see the same thing happenin' to her. Then all our dreams will be out the window.

She listened in the silence to soft halting noises Stan made and turned to cradle him in her arms.

...Lord, don't let nothin' go wrong. If anything was to happen to Sara, this man would say a prayer, then curl up and die.

Well, I'm gonna stick to her like glue 'till we find out what's what. And maybe we won't have to move. Imagine.

Sleep was out of the question. She drew a deep breath and made up her mind to watch the shadows continue their dance across the ceiling.

*** ***

Sara Morgan

Sara stepped out onto the roof and knew it was

Wednesday. All the clotheslines hung heavy, as if by common consent, this day of the week was designated wash day.

Even her mother who, back home, had always done the laundry on Monday, had fallen into the Wednesday practice.

She moved beyond the clothes lines and hurried to the rear of the building where the circle of weathered folding chairs and make-shift card table was exactly as she had left it the day before when she had come up to hear Theo practice.

...Where is he? I must tell him.

She glanced toward the lines again and decided to wait. In the early evenings when the weather was right – not too hot and not too cold- she knew that Mr. Matthew and Mr. Cyrus and a few other men from the Blind Alley played cards here.

At those times, if she sat near her bedroom window and kept very quiet, she could hear their laughter drift over the courtyard- like clouds she imagined, before floating away

The card players consumed huge amounts of beer, but the bottles and cups disappeared when they did, leaving the space ready for next time.

She gazed at the circle of chairs now and wondered why her father did not join in at least one game. One game, so she could listen to his laughter also. In the evenings, all he seemed able to do was eat supper, listen to the radio for a bit of news, then lie across the bed.

" ...is only five minutes shut-eye I gonna catch," he always said.

And he lay there on his back, smothered in layers of sweat-drenched work clothes, scuffed work shoes half unlaced, and iron-hard hands flung carelessly across his thin chest.

Last night, the knuckles were swollen and she wondered what it took to push a garment rack three times his weight day after day after day.

Once, as he slept, she thought of kneeling beside him and placing her hands across his face, lightly, to smooth the creases near his lids. She thought her fingers might re-shape the gaping mouth into the smile she needed to see, and at least diminish, if not erase entirely, the hopelessness she imagined had become his hallmark.

Then hearing her mother's voice.

"Leave him be, honey. He needs his rest.

Later is a word we share like a prayer. Talk to him later. Later, when the lawyer gets the papers straight. Later, when I graduate. Later , when we move to a nicer place. But no. Later is now. They want to move now and I'll never see Theo again.

Usually, before the card players assembled in the evening, Theo came up to practice.

To Sara, the notes he blew were clear and soft and made her dream of water. Pools and eddies and streams, narrow and deep in which she imagined herself floating as light as a grasshopper. The weightlessness made her forget the fatigue draining her father and the change that had come over her mother.

Shortly after they had moved in –Sara wasn't sure when it happened-her mother had acquired the habit of moving about as if listening for something above ordinary sound, a message expected from another wavelength. Clothilde now rarely raised her voice. Not a pot clanged as she prepared food or cleaned afterward. And her steps as she went about the house grew small and soundless.

In the evenings, as her father slept, Sara heard only the hollow click of her mother's knitting needles.

When Theo practiced, his notes slipped into this silence like a whispered invitation and it was easy to rest her head on her arms and push everything- her father's lined face, her mother's creeping silence – push it all away.

But last night, more toward morning, when she couldn't sleep, she thought she had caught a fragment of their conversation.

…For Sara. We must move for Sara. We must do this for her..

Then today, her mother wanting to know where she was going and how long she would be gone.

..To see Miss Effie, Mama. Only for an hour.

Now here she was and no sign of Theo. Yesterday, before this disaster, she had come upstairs to listen as he played three pieces back to back. Then he had paused and whispered, more to himself than to her. "I feel good when I'm up here. I can close my eyes and not think about anything while I'm playing"

"Nothing at all?" she had asked.

He had looked at her, unnerved by the light brown eyes, oval face, and the gravity of her expression. Finally, he smiled and murmured. "I didn't mean that the way it sounded."

And he returned to another solo.

Now she gazed past the heavy clotheslines without seeing them.

…he hasn't even… kissed me. Hasn't even tried..

She wondered about this feeling that pushed up inside her every time she came near him. The power of it and the fear and excitement she felt reminded her of the force of the hurricanes back home – of the winds roaring like freight engines. Roaring and then melting away to a suspended silence as if all sound and the things that made sound had gone to sleep. The eye of the storm.

Then without warning, it returned, transforming the sky into a sudden, furious gray, and driving grains of wet earth deep into her skin. She imagined herself running into the center of this sound and being swept into its turbulent core. But in reality she had scrambled for safety with her mouth full of prayer and water, choking on fear and excitement, and unable to imagine any other thing so wild and fearful.

She closed her eyes now against the parching sun in order to think through the confusion she felt whenever she connected such images with Theo.

Ah, how would I know. No matter what I do, I can't seem to get close enough to him. And if we move away, oh!!

"Sara? You up here all alone. And in this heat. You could pass out and nobody'd know you were here."

Effie Cummings, her hair covered with a blue silk scarf, moved quickly, stripping the sheets and pillow cases from her line, piled them into a basket, and then moved impatiently within the circle to sit opposite Sara.

"Heat out here is enough to make the devil faint," she sighed. Her fingers, long and thin, sorted through the bleached fabrics.

Sara relaxed. She thought of the lie she had told her mother but Effie was indeed here and so had changed it to truth. Now if only Theo would come up.

But Sara was glad to see Effie and especially glad now that she was well again.

People said something had happened at her husband's funeral, made her hair turn whiter than the towels she's folding. She must have loved him a lot. But do widows remove their wedding bands so soon...

..If anything ever happened to Theo, I'd wear mine forever.

"I was coming to see you, Miss Effie, but I thought I'd sit here and read for a few minutes.."

Effie nodded, knowing that she had come here hoping to find Theo, but said instead, "much cooler in the library, Sara. Concentrate better..."

Sara said nothing but watched Effie return the folded towels to the basket, then kick off her sandals and wriggle her toes. She had stretched out, her legs reaching beyond the small table in the center of the circle.

It was her legs, Sara decided, that had made Effie look so much taller than her husband. Mr. Cummings had seemed small and neat and overly polite, while Effie always seemed ready to reach out in some grand and disorganized fashion.

Effie's eyes were closed against the sun but Sara knew she wasn't asleep. It was too hot.

"Quite a difference from when you and your mother first showed up here," Effie said, her eyes still closed.

Sara opened her book and propped it on her head, ten-like, to shield her.

"Yes, m'am. Yes indeed. I was so cold that day, I didn't think I would ever get warm again."

She also wanted to mention that it had been Saint Valentine's Day, the day she met Theo.

*** ***

February. A two degree day when Sara stood shivering in the lobby with the two battered, rope-tied suitcases while her mother had gone upstairs to look for her father.

Effie had passed through and smiled: "Cold enough for you?"

Sara returned the smile but wondered about such a question. Her teeth were chattering and she was about to die on her first day in America. A temperature of two degrees was unimagined in Antigua.

She liked the idea of seeing so many colored faces. She liked the name, Harlem, t hat her father had written about, but the noise and grime of New York and the army of people all living so close in such large buildings made her head ache.

She had leaned back against the lobby wall, but moved quickly, shocked that marble could feel so cold. She held back the tears wondering now if leaving home had been a good idea.

When the parcel from her father had arrived, she thought he had sent a present for her 14th birthday, but wrapped within the two dresses was the envelope with the money and tickets.

Her mother, Clothilde, had leaned against the small kitchen table and hugged the letter to her, her face wet with tears.

"At last, at last, he send for us!"

Two days later, they were dressed in their gifts – Clothilde in new navy crepe and Sara in a white cotton dress with a sailor collar. Sara had crammed her feet into the cracked, toe- pinching, patent leather shoes that she hated and the next thing she knew, she was in New York where her ears, fingers, and toes ached from the sudden and terrible change.

1048 looked large and shabby and the golden streets her father had described were gray with dirty snow over which a hundred busy dogs had strayed.

The buildings appeared more solid than they actually were. All had seen better days, but 1048 was the only one taking its time about falling down. The four stories of red brick rose above a curved entrance of pink granite and if one looked carefully through the grime, a faint discoloration could be seen in the arch – evidence of a canopy that had once stretched elegantly to the curb.

Sara did not see this. She was concentrating on a strange hissing sound and shrank back against the far wall when the radiator belched a cloud of steam.

"You don't have an overcoat?" Effie had asked, extracting some letters from the mailbox. "You're playin' with double pneumonia."

"No m'am," Sara answered, not understanding what double pneumonia was. Back home, when old people had lain in their sick bed too long, their lungs filled and they sometimes died of pneumonia. But double pneumonia? Maybe in America, they named everything twice, like New York New York.

She wanted to ask but the woman had already gone upstairs leaving her alone again.

The radiator made more sounds, louder and more threatening and Sara expected an explosion. Before she could decide which way to run, her mother and the woman re-appeared at the top of the stairs.

"I could tell from the way you all were dressed," Effie said, introducing herself and extending a heavy sweater to Sara" I could tell how you're all decked out in those summer outfits that you're related to the gentleman in 3B. He left early this morning. Come on up to my place and make yourself at home. He'll be in soon."

In Effie Cummings' living room, Sara stared at a sofa large enough to have filled two rooms back home. In the bathroom, she moved her fingers over the blue tiled walls and oversized tub and gazed at the toilet that emptied at the press of a handle.

And what an extravagance to have a small rug laid over a carpet that covered the entire living room floor so that no wood showed. Not even a splinter.

"No, child," Effie smiled when Sara was comfortable enough to finally ask questions. "There are no streets of gold. I've lived here all my life and haven't seen one yet. Only thing is work and more work and most people trying to make do. And weekends, lots of dances and parties to help folks forget how hard they had to scuffle to make it to the weekend in the first place".

She turned to Clothilde. "Well, it's not really that bad. And once you get settled, ask your husband to take you to the Club Harlem on 145th Street. Fancy place. I didn't go there too often because the Savoy down on Lenox was my favorite spot..."

But Sara had wanted to hear about the Apollo, the theatre her father had written about. She wanted to hear about Pig Meat Markham, Buck and Bubbles, Moms Mabley, and especially the Red Fox who had made her father laugh so hard, he had hiccups for two days.

"..Now that is really the place. It stays packed, especially on Wednesdays for amateur night. Sometimes they have to put up barricades. I used to go all the time before I got married..Saw Ella Fitzgerald on the show. She was supposed to do a dance number but these two dancers had come on before her and brought down the house so she figured she couldn't follow that act and win. She changed up and came on singing."

Effie shook her head remembering events and people Sara had never heard of.

"The Savoy has a beautiful mirrored globe in the ceiling and when it turns, it's like diamonds are floating in the air, and the diamonds skim over your dress, sparkling. Makes you feel like a queen... like a queen when you're dancing.."

"I used to go there a lot, especially on Thursday nights. We called it Pot Wrestler's Night and Kitchen Mechanics' Night because all the cooks and maids workin' for the rich folks got that day off. And they'd get all dressed up and head straight for the Savoy. You never saw dancin' 'till you've been there on a Thursday night. But like I said, for me, that was a while ago."

Effie's voice was low and throaty and did not seem to match her soft features. Sara liked her tall slim figure and the rich sounds she made when she laughed. She also liked the hot chocolate she served even if it wasn't as strong as the cocoa tea her mother made back home.

She tried to follow the conversation, but Effie was speaking so fast about so many things and that bumpy Pan Am flight had made it impossible for her to close her eyes so now, despite her mother's disapproving glance, she fell asleep.

She woke when the door slammed and it took some seconds to remember where she was. A thin brown man walked into the living room, leaned over Effie's chair and absently touched the side of

her face. "How are you, dear?"

He sounded so formal and Sara wondered if he would have spoken at all if she and her mother had not been there.

Effie, who had been talking so fast before Sara had fallen asleep, now seemed to have slowed down. She sounded different, slightly anxious.

"This is Mrs. Morgan and her daughter, Sara. Mrs. Morgan, this is my husband, Maxwell Cummings."

Sara had been taught to say 'pleased to meet you' but as she shook Mr. Cummings' hand, she was not so sure. His palm and fingers were soft, like Miss Jamison's, the school mistress back home but his eyes were like black arrows.

"So, you're here for a visit?"

"Yes sir," Sara whispered, glancing at her mother for a cue.

But her mother remained silent, watching him politely.

"Well," he said finally, "enjoy your stay."

" –Supper's ready," Effie said as her husband made his way toward the bedroom. "All I have to – "

"No. No. I don't have time. A committee meeting's been scheduled – "

"Another meeting?"

Through the open door, Sara watched him take two suits from the closet and lay them on the bed. It was as if Effie had not spoken. Sara watched him intently and was disappointed when her mother said, "perhaps I should see if my husband's come in. Thank you for allowing – "

"It was no bother. None at all," Effie said in her changed voice.

What a pretty lady, Sara thought. Just looked a little cloudy when her husband came in, that's all.

At the door, Sara returned the sweater and noticed that Effie's shoulders seemed to slope when she folded it in her arms.

In the hall, the suitcases seemed heavier as she and her mother struggled up the stairs. It did not occur to her that Mr. Cummings had not offered to help until she heard a voice behind her. "Lemme hold that, Miss."

Without a word, she released her suitcase into the hands of a tall young man with sandy brown hair and the nicest eyes she had ever seen.

He took both cases and continued up the steps behind them."Y'all new here?"

Sara could not answer. She was trying not to gaze at his eyes.

Her mother replied that they were indeed new here and would he please handle the bags carefully as there were some important and delicate things inside.

The young man, who introduced himself as Theo Paige, looked at the frayed rope holding the cases and tried not to smile. Sara caught his expression and looked away, too embarrassed to speak.

*** ***

It really had been a two-degree day, Sara thought, remembering the cold that had settled in her marrow and which had taken weeks to dissolve.

Now, whenever Theo wanted to tease her, he'd ask about the sailor-collared dress and those cracked, patent-leather shoes.

She adjusted the book and concentrated on the flock of pigeons circling high over 8th Avenue. They spiraled away in a rush, then swooped low, caw cawing sounds fading in their wake.

She thought of the bright colored sea-going birds that nested on the reefs back home. When a wave broke, the birds rose on large languid wings to hang suspended above the white flume and a moment later, settle again in the quiet cove. She remembered the changeless rhythm of the birds and the fine mist the breeze left on her face.

She touched her face now as the caw-cawing sounds returned. The pigeons flew in a widening arc, and then disappeared once more, as if the hard heat was too burdensome for their pale gray wings.

"You're right, Miss Effie." Sara had spoken before the words had hardly formed in her mind. "The library will be much cooler."

Chapter Ten

THEOPAIGE

"Young man, if you persist in talking, you'll have to leave," the librarian whispered, frowning behind her desk..

"Yes m'am. We were just leaving."

"But you just got here," Sara whispered, looking around her. "Where'll we go?"

"I don't know. Let's just walk..."

She hesitated. After all, she had told her mother that she was going to the library, not on a sightseeing trip. Two lies in one day were too much.

She wanted to discuss this but the librarian was staring, so she closed her book and followed Theo out of the building.

Lenox Avenue was a maze of shoppers, children, strollers, and a line of baby carriages. Families lounged on stoops in a futile attempt to escape the heat of crowded apartments.

The record shop across the avenue played 'Pledging My Love,' the latest hit by Johnny Ace and the lyrics competed with the restlessness of a crowd gathered on the opposite side.

They nodded and cheered as speaker after speaker denounced Senator McCarthy.

"...Every Negro who stands up for his rights is seen as a threat to this government," one orator shouted. "Now our artists, our actors, our writers, are losing what few jobs they had because someone accused them of being Communists. What is a Communist anyway?

"Well, it must be something good," he went on without waiting for an answer, "because those same government folks who ought to know better is falling all over themselves selling good old U.S. of A. farm machinery to them. Supposed to be surplus. Never mind the poor Negro farmer who's still struggling behind his broken down mule.

"And never mind that he can't even show his face in a bank for a loan to improve his situation. If he showed up, he'd be a threat!"

The crowd erupted in a roar and more listeners joined the gathering. Sara wanted to hear more but Theo knew that his father or Cyrus frequently joined these crowds, so he eased her away.

"Miss Effie told me..." he began. His voice was low, as though he were still in the library, and his remark was swallowed in the sounds of the street.

They turned on to 7th Avenue and strolled past Small's Paradise where workmen were taking down posters of Billy Eckstine and putting up new ones for Sarah Vaughn's show.

"My Pop used to play here," Theo said as they stopped to read the lineup.

"At Small's?" Sara asked, cupping her hand against the glass to peer inside. It was dark but she could make out the thin silhouettes of chairs stacked upside down on the elegantly shaped oak bar.

A porter was mopping the floor near the bandstand and Theo wanted to step in to ask him if he knew Matthew Paige, the great sax player, but changed his mind. Sara would know he was showing off.

...well, one day, I'm gonna play here. And at Minton's and at Birdland and it won't be no show-off. It'll be real. Just like my Pop.

They moved away from the window and he began to whistle but the notes sounded low and dry. The one thing he wanted most was to sit down and remain in one place for more than five minutes with her. He needed to know how she felt about things. About him. But that never happened. Something or someone always interrupted.

He stopped whistling, drew a deep breath, but was still unable to speak.

...The few times we were on the roof, we hadn't been alone two minutes before her mother or Miss Effie or Miss Rose came up complaining about the heat. Or Pop and his buddies settled in to play cards. Something was always gettin'in the way.

.. Even now. In the library, how did that lady with those cola bottle glasses even know it was me talkin' anyway?

He stole a glance at Sara as they strolled. The elastic top of her peasant blouse was down a little and the sun played against her bare brown shoulders. He heard the squeak of her straw sandals with each step she took.

She was nearly as tall as he was and so slim, he knew he could encircle her waist with both hands. If he ever got the chance.

...but what would he say? All those phrases he'd practiced before his mirror and perfected in the lunchroom last term sounded stupid now. It was summer. School was out. His boys were scattered on vacation and all those words that had seemed so hip were, after all, just words.

So there had been no other way to connect except through his music. Play in the window and let the notes catch in the air to drift through the bricks and the blinds and the curtains. That way he could call her name with a sharp, or a bass note to let her know what he felt and how his chest tightened when he glanced up and saw her curtain move when a solo ended. He needed to tell her these things.

His hands were sweating and he jammed them in the pockets of his khaki trousers. Finally he managed to say, "uhm, do you think we could go to the movies one of these days?"

They strolled half a block before she answered. "When?"

"I don't know. Next Saturday, maybe? I hear there's an Oscar Micheaux flick at the Odeon. And 'Cabin In The Sky' with Lena Horne"

"Cabin In The Sky' is an old film."

"You seen it already?"

"No."

"Well?"

She did not answer immediately, but lifted her shoulders slightly as if trying to make up her mind. "Well, maybe. If I'm not doing anything."

That meant she would ask her mother and if it was okay, she would go. He felt his chest expand and he wanted to open his mouth wide, to take in air.

...well, Pop was right. The first step on any road is always the hardest...

They walked for several blocks and he saw nothing except the dark interior of the Odeon Theatre with vague images flickering across the screen. He imagined his hands on her shoulders, her peasant blouse down even lower, and his mouth where her brassiere should have been and he would not have raised his head if Lena Horne herself had stepped from the screen and called his name.

"Theo?"

"Huh?"

"You're not listening? I said I heard something the other night."

"Something.like what?"

She looked up. Her wide eyes held his reflection. "I heard my father say – I heard him say we might be moving."

"What??"

"I don't know for sure. Maybe I was dreaming. I think I heard it but I'm too afraid to ask."

The small voice and song-like accent trailed away leaving a vacuum in which he heard only the hammering of his own heart. He stared dumbly, as if she had spoken a language he could not comprehend. Then she spoke again:

"Theo, oh Theo. I'm afraid." She came close and he felt the ground shift. She touched him and her fingers were like tiny sparks on his arm.

"You're moving??" he repeated. "Moving?"

Before she could answer, he had reached out. His grip was too tight and his hands too clumsy, but he pressed her to him and closed his eyes. Closed out the rush and tide of people; the cars, bicycles, strollers and roller skaters. The doleful sounds of Johnnie Ace mourning a lost love. The memory of the speakers railing against the government dimmed. He shut out the candesence of the mid-day sun so that only her image burned before him.

"No. Oh. No," was all he could manage. And his mouth found hers because the words he needed most at that moment would not come.

Chapter Eleven
APT 3B

Clothilde drummed her fingers on the kitchen table, clasped them together as if in prayer, then stared at Sara.

"Girl, what is wrong with you? I send you to the library for readin' and you runnin' the streets kissin' up the boys? If your daddy get wind of this, he gonna beat the skin off your behind. Oh, looka my troubles this day, oh Lord. Look, Jesus."

Sara had been chatting aimlessly with her mother about the heat, the noise of the crowded streets, and anything else that came to mind, except Theo and how beautiful his music made her feel. Now she sat back, dumbfounded. How had this news reached home before she did. Who saw her. Who told...

"Mama please. May I say – "

"No! And another thing! Why he didn't come callin' like a proper young man? What he think I'm raisin' in my house, enh? Well, you know what? I'm gonna have a talk with his mama and let her know where I'm standin' on certain criterions. Meanwhile , young missy, if you want to see the inside of any college, you better mind and keep your skirt down and your knees together, you hear what I'm tellin ' you??"

"Yes m'am. I understand. Yes." Sara stared at the floor. She felt her heart sink. This was terrible. Terrible. Now they would probably move for sure.

How did all this happen. One kiss. One kiss...

But it wasn't one kiss. It was the heart of the hurricane she had been reaching for all along and it had taken her away. Theo's arms had touched her and his mouth had felt strange and familiar and peppermint sweet.

Clothilde was still talking and Sara wondered if she had missed anything.

".And how you let this happen ? All your business spread out in a public place. You. A properly raised girl. I knew these American boys were too fast, fast, fast..."

"But, Mama, it didn't happen the way you think. No. Not the way you think. Theo, he, he hugged me because I was upset. I was upset and he was trying to calm me."

Clothilde's hand slammed down on the table, rattling the sugar bowl. "Bring me a better tale, missy. What was you so upset about that the vagabond had to smother you in broad daylight on 135th Street and 7th Avenue, enh? Answer me that?"

Sara wished she could tell her mother that it was really 139th Street. They had been walking along Strivers Row, a street thick with the rich green of the trees that lined the curb, the low hanging branches shading balconies of fine filigree and she had been swept away with the idea of someday living in one of these fine homes with Theo, the man she loved.

That's where and when and how it happened and if someone was going to carry a tale, the least they could have done was carry it straight.

Instead, she lowered her gaze again. "I told him.. I told him..that I thought we might be moving – "

Clothilde pressed her hands to her head and closed her eyes. "Ah, no! Not only is the girl bold and shameless but she nosey too. Got her ear plastered up to her bedroom door in the middle of the night when she should be sleepin'. Then she go carryin' the family news all about like a town crier. Ah, Lord, look at my troubles. Look and tell me if I deserve this shabby treatment from my own child."

"Mama, please – "

"No. You listen." Clothilde rose and began to move around the table, forgetting her usual measured steps. "Since you playin' FBI, yes we thinkin' of movin' 'cause of that convict just come outta prison. With him in the place, the authorities will come nosin' around and we don't need none of that. Now, with you carryin' on with no shame, we don't need none of that either.

"How you expect me to hold up my head with you scandalizin' we family name? Yes, we movin' but I gonna speak to that woman and let her know what kind of son she raisin'."

Sara struggled to her feet. This was all too much. Everything was going wrong. Not to see him. Or speak to him. Moving away from him. She put her hands to her mouth and leaned against the table, shaking. It was the hurricane again and she had no control but this time she wanted to scream.

Clothilde stopped pacing and stared. "Girl, you shakin' like a leaf. Get hold of yourself. And dry them tears. Your eyes'll be all red when your daddy walk in the door, and he will know in a minute that something is wrong with you."

She moved to the stove and put on a pot of tea, then in a softer voice, continued. "What you must understand is that your daddy is makin' a big sacrifice for you, Sara. A big sacrifice. Would you have a chance to go to school if we was back home?

"All we asking is for you to take advantage of something' me and him never had. You see how he drags himself in here every night, half dead. He's killin' himself for you. For you, girl."

Sara continued to cry as Clothilde placed the cups on the table. "Come. Come. You floodin' the place out. Bawlin' like as if the movin' van is downstairs already. Hush up and lemme think about this some more…"

Clothilde gazed at her daughter across the table, watching the sunlight dance over the smooth brow, the large almond shaped brown eyes and the black hair pulled back in a long pony tail. She looked in the girl's eyes and saw herself from years ago.

Beautiful. Not knowing, and all at once felt a crushing pain spiral in her chest.

…Maybe it was just one kiss. But how can I stop this. How. Nobody stopped me… I must speak to that boy's mother.

Chapter Twelve
APT2A

" 'The Glory of Love' by the Five Keys drifted in soft alto from the small radio on the shelf above the kitchen sink.

Matthew clicked the sound off and ground out his cigarette so hard, it snapped in two.

"Look, boy, I expect you to be up front with me. Mrs. Morgan would not have been so upset if 'nothing happened' as you say. Now your mother's upset and saying that you manhandled Sara in the street like a common hoodlum. Don't tell me nothing happened."

Theo shifted from one foot to the other. He had never seen his father so angry. "Well, I mean… I mean, it didn't exactly happen the way Mrs Morgan said it did."

"How did it happen?"

"To tell you the truth I…don 't know. It.. just happened."

Matthew stared at his son. The anger shifted and a vague unease rose in his chest. He lit another cigarette and quickly snuffed it out. "Listen, Theo, you might as well sit down 'cause this is gonna take awhile. Now it's true I haven't said too much to you about life and all that stuff, but this is as good a time as any.

"I know how you feel about Sara. And I think I know how she feels about you. After all, that curtain upstairs ain't exactly movin' by itself, is it?"

He ignored Theo's shocked silence and went on. "I mean I seen the power of love move a lot of things, but curtains wasn't one of them."

Theo's silence gave way to a nervous smile and he put his hands in his pockets and slouched down in the kitchen chair.

"Aw, Pop. Aw."

At least the boy was listening so Matthew's tone softened.

"You know, when your mother and I got married, we were in love too but it wasn't easy. Hard times knocked on the door, walked in and made itself right at home. Took forever to invite 'im out again.

"Some weeks it was hand to mouth with nothing in the hand.

"We want it to be different for you. You want to be a lawyer. We're damn proud of that. We really are. If you want to become another Thurgood Marshall, you can but that's hard work. You can't get sidetracked. I mean Sara is a nice girl but her folks have plans for her too. She wants to go to medical school. Don't ruin it for both of you by bringing a baby here before you can take care of it."

"A baby?? A baby?? Dad, I only- "

Matthew held up his hand. "That's what they all say. 'I only. I only, and the next thing you know, here comes an invitation to the christening."

He reached into his pocket and placed several small round cellophane packets on the table between them. "Listen, I hope you take my advice and think twice before you find yourself in a deal where you gonna use this, but if the situation comes up, I don't want you playin'in the rain without a raincoat. Any girl you get in trouble-not just Sara but any girl – you gonna stand before the preacher and do the right thing. And son, if you ain't in love, you facin' eighteen years of hard domestic labor with no reprieve. If you are in love, then it's just eighteen years with no hopes, no nuthin' except a dream about how your life could have been.

"You gonna be watchin' Mr. Marshall on the T.V. and lookin' sideways at your kid, hopin' for a better life for him."

Theo listened, feeling the heat rise to his face as he gazed at the packets. He thought of Big Mouth Bee-Jay, the youngest and smallest guy in the group, who couldn't make the basketball squad no matter how hard he scuffled, so he bragged about how good he was at other things.

And everyone believed him until the night they were hanging out around the street lamp trying to out-drift the Drifters and Bee-Jay took the lead, throwing up his hands to grandstand before the girls on the stoop and the packet slipped out of his shirt pocket. When he bent to retrieve it, the rubber had been so dry, it cracked.

"Your poppa must gave you that the daa..ay you were born," the lead man sang in a rolling bass. The girls laughed and pinched each other.

To compound the humiliation, the alto chimed in, high, clear, a-cappella: "And it..it look to me..ee like you ain't git a chance to uuuu....use it yet."

Theo wondered if Bee-Jay, after that night, had ever replaced it or if he just decided to take his chances.

The packets were spread out on the table in a small semi-circle and he prayed his mother would not walk in on this conversation. What would he say to her? What could he say to his father, sitting across from him preparing to light another cigarette as coolly as if they had been discussing the weather.

He made up his mind. If his mother walked in, he would simplify things and slide under the table and die. But right now, he had to deal with his father.

"Dad, listen. I'm not gonna get sidetracked. I understand what you're saying and I'm sorry about what happened. I guess I got a little off balance because of what Sara told me."

"What did she say?"

Theo was quiet and Matthew concentrated on the spiral of smoke rising from the ashtray and waited. He could see that whatever it was, was too painful to contemplate.

"They might be- they might be going away." Theo lifted his shoulders. "Her folks said something about it not being safe. Safe for who? For them? For Sara?"

He turned to look at his father. "Dad, that's the same thing Mom told me last week: 'it's not safe. Every day now, she wants to know where I'm going and how long I'll be gone and stuff like that. She never asked me before. I always knew I had to be in the house by such and such a time. Now I practically have to draw a map for her to put pins in. I don't know what's going on."

"I'll tell you what's going on," Matthew said quietly. "It's that Rhino."

"What? What does that creep have to do with me?" He's so mean, he doesn't even rate a hello."

Matthew gazed at his son and then looked away. He wondered how old Seaweed would have been and who would be taking care of him now.

"It's a long story, Theo. A long story. One of these days, when your mother feels up to it, she'll tell you. But let's get back to first things first. What are you going to do about this problem with Mrs. Morgan?"

Theo lowered his eyes. "Unh, I don't know. "

"You are going to knock on her door and you are going to apologize, that's what you're going to do. You're going to let her know you meant no disrespect to her daughter."

Matthew watched Theo hesitate so he added quickly, "if you don't, I can guarantee you won't get within waving distance of that girl again."

Theo nodded and moved from the table. Matthew reached for his hand. "Wait a minute. For God's sake, leave all that stuff here. Suppose one falls out your pocket while you're pleading your case. You want the woman to have a heart attack? Seems like I gotta tell you everything!"

He reached into his trouser pocket again and brought out two dollars. "Here. Stop by the florist and ask Mr. Atkins to fix up a nice bunch of roses or something. Make sure you give them to the mother, not the daughter, you understand? If things work out, and she doesn't kick you out, there'll be plenty of chances later on to buy flowers for Sara."

The door closed and Matthew was alone in the kitchen. His mouth felt dry and he knew he was smoking too much.

...first, this thing with Theo. Now the Morgans are planning to cut out. They can't be that scared of Rhino. They don't even know him yet. Damn! This is all Sandra needs to hear and she'll start hollering again for us to move too. Damn!

He needed to talk and wondered whether Cyrus was up to sharing a bourbon.

Chapter Thirteen
THE WEEKEND

AL & AL
says
It's Friday!
Come on all
Let's have a ball
Leave your troubles
In the hall
Taste our whiskey
Wine and gin
Red rice, trotters
(it's a sin)
Just a dollar
Let's you holler
Party ends
When you say when!!

On weekends, night does not close in. It glides over like a soft and necessary slipcover discreetly hiding the damage of a hard existence. Friday's fading light sweeps across kitchen tables, blurring stacks of accumulated bills. The same fading light moves up narrow halls into small rented rooms where it accentuates the 'AL & AL', 'Sweets & Mary' and 'Sweet Dee' printed party cards wedged loosely in the mirror frame on the dresser.

And week-end darkness, thick with expectation, brings into sharp relief the glowing marquees of the Rennie Ballroom, the Rockland Palace, the Apollo, Smalls Paradise, the Peacock, and the Savoy.

Soul and spirit revive knowing this is the time to step. Lay-away outfits are laid out. Baths are perfumed. Hair is styled not by any ordinary middle- of- the- week hairdresser who made do with a hot comb in a hot kitchen, but by Landeros in his orchid and antique filled Sugar Hill salon and who drove a dark lavender Cadillac convertible on his days off. Women waved as he cruised by, his silver pomaded hair glowing in the breeze.

Midnight:

Seventh Avenue is a parade. Those souls who had held back, who purposely waited a few hours now step out fast and light to effect breathless entrances into Jock's Place, Shalimar's, or the Red Rooster. One drink later, they re-join the parade and move on to the jazz scene at Minton's or to Connie's, rushing now to catch up with whatever they imagined they might have missed earlier.

Midnight in the Blind Alley.

Blue listened to Matthew's solo float over the half empty dance floor. He waited until the band left the stage for a break, and then plugged in the jukebox. Fats Domino's echo sounded hollow as he found his thrill on blueberry hill and Blue wondered if he should have turned on the box at all.

The door opened and Cyrus walked in as Matthew approached the bar. "I know August is supposed to be slow but this is serious," Cyrus remarked. "where's the action?"

"That's what I'd like to know," Blue said, filling some bowls with salted peanuts and potato chips for the few patrons present. Salt created thirst and thirst created sales. Hopefully.

"Matt and me was just talkin' about it earlier. Anything special happening anywhere? Some big get together we don't know about?"

Cyrus ordered a bourbon. "The only thing I saw out of the ordinary was Rhino. Hugging up the stoop like he thinks the place gonna fall down if he step off."

"Shit. No wonder the joint's dead. Folks are afraid to move past him," Blue said. "Same thing happened last week. What? He thinks his life's mission is to ugly up the stoop? If that's the case, I may as well vacation for the duration."

He carried the small bowls to the tables and returned to fold his arms on the counter. Fats Domino faded and the Platters came on, but this time only three couples got up to dance.

Blue gazed at them wondering what his night's take would look like and if he would have enough to pay the band.

"Look, Rhino's been out, what is it, over three weeks, nearly a month now and nothing's happened. He wasn't supposed to stay here, remember? What's the word?"

"Ain't heard," Matt said. "We've been talking to Mrs. Dillard but the way she sounds, I think he's got her jumping at her own shadow."

"She knows," Cyrus added, "that Rhino's persona non grata, but – "

"Person a what?" Blue had opened a beer and put it down.

"Don't tell me the damn fool went and got something else wrong with him?"

'It means he's unwelcome," Matt said.

"Well I should think so if he got that kind of condition," Blue sighed. "Too much strange stuff goin' round as it is. And God knows that boy don't need nothing else latching on to him.

"You know, from the time that boy opened his eyes and looked in the mirror, he ain't been nothing but trouble. Wished he'd been my kid. All this mess never would have happened. I'd have brought him up right or killed him trying. "

He moved to the end of the bar to serve a customer, leaving Matthew and Cyrus to drink in silence.

Matthew leaned against the bar and watched the few couples glide across the slightly raised platform that served as the dance floor. They moved in and out of the shadows, bodies in sync, wholly absorbed in each other. Even when the record ended, they remained together, poised for the next selection to slip down the spindle.

The couples whispered and waited and a woman laughed softly into her partner's ear. Was she buoyed by the press of his weight against her or by the Brilliantine fragrance of his Saturday night haircut?

The needle hit the record and the Harptones came on with "A Sunday Kind Of Love." Matthew raised his glass and thought of Sandra. He wished he could hear her laugh. He'd even settle for a thin smile. Lately, she had become more and more upset each time she heard Rhino's name.

Cyrus cut into his reverie. "Well, I don't want to say that we're stuck but we may have to wait until he does something, you know, maybe violate his parole or something. Beyond that, all we can do is try to keep an eye on him."

"You think that's gonna mean anything," Matthew asked. "Keeping an eye on him? He's been stared at all his life."

"Here we go again," Blue said, returning to catch the tail end of the conversation. He threw up his hands in disgust. "You always trying to take up for him. Blaming society and shit like that. We can't help it if he came out the oven before he browned up. Ain't our fault. He got beef, take it to The Man upstairs. I say the cat is wrong and when he's wrong, damn it, he's wrong!"

"All right. All right, we ain't got to get testy," Matthew said. "I feel as bad about it as you do. But we've been stepping round this question too long. It's time to pee or get off the pot."

"You know what Rhino's problem is," Blue continued, opening a new bottle of beer. "His problem is he ain't a 'roon."

Cyrus looked at him. "What the hell is that? I never heard of it."

"Oh, that's like your persona-whatever," Blue said. "Anyway, you know how The Man divided us up back in slavery times. You had your pure African, then somebody got slick and invented the mulatto; then they threw in somethin' funny called the quadroon, then they come with up the octoroon. And on and on till all them 'roons got everybody real confused.

"Now anybody taking one peep at me ain't gonna get confused . No sir. But the way the folks got it programmed, I'm supposed to jump salty when somebody calls me Blue. Hell, I know who I am and damn proud of it. On the other hand now, Rhino – who ain't even a sixteenth of a 'roon is whiter than a bowl of Carolina rice and mad as hell about it."

Cyrus ordered another bourbon and shook his head. "That's why he's so obsessed with Rose."

"That's a wild theory," Matthew said.

"I don't know theory from diddly," Blue answered. "I only know that Rose kinda looks just like his mama when his mama was a kid. Same skin, eyes, everything. Y'all can't see it 'cause you so close to her but Rhino sure 'nough sees it. Or thinks he does. Now he's hangin' ugly, lookin' like he on a steady diet of bat burgers. I'm tellin' you it's enough to scare the shit out a blind man."

"How would he know what his mama looks like? She cut out even before he came home from the hospital," Matthew said.

"Well who knows? Maybe he saw a picture or something."

The phone rang and Blue picked it up on the second ring. "Evening. This is the Alley. Blind when you stroll in, stone blind when you roll out. What can I do for you? Yeah? Hey Rose, we were just – no, he's right here. Hold on."

Cyrus grabbed the receiver, nodded, and quickly hung up.

"Be back in a minute. Rose just came from the Apollo. She's across the street in the Peacock, too scared to come into the house because of that damn – "

He slammed his hand on the counter surprising both Blue and Matthew. "That damn Rhino thinks he can bulldoze everybody, he's got another thought coming."

"No. Wait a minute, Cyrus. Don't get your pressure up. Lemme walk out with you."

"No, Matthew. She's my niece, my responsibility. Besides, I'm not going to blows with him. I'm just going to get Rose."

Blue placed a napkin over Cyrus's glass. "Well, you know how to holler if you need backup. Ain't no sense pullin'no solo showdown."

The door had barely closed and Matthew said, "Blue, I'll give him one minute, then I'm out after him. Tell the guys to go on. I'll be right back."

"Now ain't this some shit!"

"I know. I know, but what we gonna do? Right now I think Cyrus ought to send Rose out of town for a while. At least till we can settle this thing."

"Well, why don't we all just go away," Blue said, his anger rising. "Why don't we all just disappear and leave the whole damn house. I could close this joint, lay in the cut and wait till I hear that Rhino had died of old age or something. Yeah. Let's do that."

Matthew sighed as he walked toward the door. "We'll talk when I get back. Tell the guys to tune up. Break's over."

Blue glanced at his watch as the door closed a second time. A minute later, he signaled for Francine, one of the regulars, to take his place behind the bar. He glanced at the pistol but decided to leave it on the shelf.

Chapter Fourteen
SHOWDOWN

Rhino leaned against the iron railing on the stoop and watched Cyrus, and then Matthew brush past. Both glanced his way – he thought he saw Matthew frown – but neither of them spoke to him.

His fingers curled around the wrought iron spikes as he watched them stroll across 8th avenue and enter the Peacock.

…Think they goin' to have a good time…Matt and his sad ass music, and that dumb Cyrus. They ain't shit. ..

He watched the neon bird over the entrance blink through its vivid procession of color and grew more angry as the seconds passed.

…where is she? Where the hell is she?

That morning, he had followed Rose downtown on the subway, waited across the street from the factory and watched her go to lunch with her friends and return. He heard her laughter drift toward him. Her blue print dress and straw sandals wavered like a bold banner in the garment center crowd. He counted the hours.

Five o'clock, the doors opened again and the workers poured out, heading home. He followed her to the "A" train, then watched from the window of the adjoining car.

But at 125th street, something happened. She must have changed her mind about something and gotten off the train and quickly headed for the exit.

He tried to catch up, pushing and cursing and tearing his way through the turnstile and people stared as he was pinned against the wall by a pair of dark, oversized, policemen.

"What's your rush, buddy? You running to something or from something?"

He saw her blue dress and straw sandals disappear up the stairs and was suddenly so blinded by anger that he could not put two words together to tell the police what he thought of them – to scream at them for keeping him from her – that everyone was keeping him from her, and that that was the real reason they had put him in prison, not for Tommy, but to keep him away from her.

They held him for ten minutes in the small air-less room near the change booth until he finally stopped shaking, then let him go with a warning: "Don't be pulling nothing funny 'cause you know you ain't too hard to spot. Be cool, if you know what's good for you!"

Once out of the subway, he had moved slowly, without seeing, but knowing that if someone had bumped into him, or stepped on his toe, he would have killed them without a word.

At home, he ignored his grandmother's questioning stare and quickly closed himself in the bathroom. Across the courtyard, Rose's windows were dark. He cursed again and raced back downstairs to hold to the stoop's iron railing as if he were clutching the blade of a knife.

...She might be in the Peacock. Smilin' at them smart-ass sommabitches with the big rings and suits. Oughtta get me a gun, bust in and spray the whole damn place. Clear everybody out. Every damn one of 'em.

But he knew he could never do that. He could not go near there now, not as long as the peacock's tail feathers still lit randomly out of sequence and not as long as he was unable to figure out why.

...Can't fool me. They did that on purpose. They did that for...

The lobby door creaked on its hinges and he turned to see Blue standing behind him.

"Look here, Rhino, I want a word.."

"About what?"

" - A lot of stuff, but some of it can wait. Right now, I need to talk about the Alley."

"What about it? I ain't in it."

"No, but you damn close."

"What's that supposed to mean?"

"It means you crimping my style, hanging like this. Folks thinking twice about stepping in."

Rhino leaned against the railing and gazed at Blue, then started to laugh. "Case you ain't heard the word yet, this is a free country. I stand anywhere I feel like. Anywhere, you understand? You ain't got customers? Folks ain't comin' to the party? Maybe they sick a that rot-gut whisky and sad-ass music you all the time dishin' up. That's your problem and you tryin' to hang it on me? Hell, no. I ain't goin' nowhere. This is a free country."

Blue glanced around. A few persons strolled past the stoop, nodded and headed down the block. A taxi slowed, picked up a fare, made a U turn and sped off.

Standing there, Blue could feel the floating excitement peculiar to Friday nights. Despite his anger, it managed to settle on him almost like a perfume. Under different circumstances, he would have breathed in deeply, then perhaps strolled a couple of blocks along the avenue, maybe drop into the Midway or the 19th Hole, where the crowd knew him and he would set up the bar, slap the manager on the back, and hang around a minute or so listening to the juke box spill some of Little Richard's hard time testimonials.

All that was good for business but with Rhino holding up traffic, it would be wasted. Any minute now, Matthew and Cyrus would be stepping out of the Peacock. He needed to cut this conversation .

He reached out suddenly and grabbed Rhino by his shirt.

"Listen, we ain't gittin' in no hot debate about no freedom shit, you understand? You free to stand where you can. But let's see you do it with a fuckin' broken leg.

He twisted the shirt tightly, pulling Rhino to him, then quickly let go, pushing him back against the railing.

"And you talkin' that talk about my whisky? About my music? I ought to knot your fuckin' head on general principles, for not knowin' what a good drink taste like and what real music sound like. I ought to do you a favor and whip some culture into your ass!"

He moved forward again but Rhino quickly side-stepped him and darted off the stoop, his lean shoulders drawn tight as a street cat.

"Yeah! Go on and try, you midnight mothafucka! You got to keep smilin' just so people can see you!"

He said this as he backed away, remaining just out of reach." You got to keep smilin'!" he yelled.

Blue shrugged and leaned against the door. "That's right, mothafucka. I sure do smile. Especially when my daddy and my mama call me by my name, which is more than yours ever did. I smile a lot. And if I catch you on this stoop again, I'm a smile some more while I whip your imitation rice-a-roni, rice puddin' ass, black and blue."

"We gonna see about that," Rhino answered. He turned away, slowly, trying to make it appear as if he had the upper hand, the last word but as he moved away, Blue's laughter trailed in his wake like a shadow he could not out run.

*** ***

Chapter Fifteen
ROSE

Rose stared at the ground as Cyrus and Matthew escorted her across the avenue. The noise of passing cars and the music from Miss Laura's All Nite Luncheonette competed with the sounds from the Peacock and filled the air with a humming which at other times would not have bothered her. Hearing it now made her dizzy.

The stoop was empty and she wanted to believe that Rhino might have played only in her imagination but then Matthew whistled, "bird sure know when to fly the coop.."

"Yep. Can't stand still for the big game," Cyrus said.

And her earlier sudden surprise and fright turned to anger. In the lobby, Matthew said goodnight and disappeared into the darkness of the alley, leaving Cyrus to escort her upstairs. Now each step, each turn she took on the landing crystallized her rage. In her apartment, Cyrus poured two glasses of bourbon and handed one to her.

"Listen, Rose, I've been thinking..."

He began to pace the floor and Rose waited, knowing that whatever he was about to say would not be good. She turned her glass around and around in her hand, studying the simple design near the rim.

"...Rose, what do you say to the idea of going away. Just for a while, until we can get a handle on this situation with Rhino. I don't –"

Rose placed her glass on the table and was on her feet before he finished. "Im not going anywhere. I belong here. I got plans and nobody's gonna sidetrack me. I'm gonna- "

She sat down and reached for the glass.

...Tommy had the plans, not me. And he was sidetracked. Murdered. Didn't even get a chance to hear me at the Apollo. Didn't even get a chance...

Cyrus moved about the room , and she tried not to acknowledge the fear etched in his frown.

But I'm gonna do it. I gotta do it. Tommy said that once I started singing, everything would come my way. And I believe him. I still believe it.

Besides, how could Cyrus know what it's like in that hot, stinking, factory day in and day out with those locked doors and windows and you practically choking to death on all that dust the machines throwing off. I must have stitched a collar on every damn blouse in the world. I'm getting outta there, but I'm not leaving town to do it.

Cyrus was speaking, softly she knew, so as not to upset her. He was speaking logically so that she could see clearly the wisdom of whatever he was proposing. She heard not a word but wondered how she had been so unprepared for this.

She had formed the habit of carrying the pearl handled razor in her purse, not as a talisman or a weapon but as a reminder of nights when she had lain in the steaming, perfumed water, watching Tommy as he looked in the mirror and angled the pearl handle against his cheek, gliding the blade around his ear, under his neck, and the shaving cream disappearing with each light stroke. And his smile when he whispered. "Don't want to bruise my baby," and smiling when he eased into the water to lay atop her. "Aah, is this smooth enough? Baby, is it soft enough?

And the water rising almost to the rim, so that she had to hold her chin up.

. "Aaah. Yes. It's smooth enough, honey. I don't need it soft, though. You know mama can't use it soft. Oh!"

Her knees were wide and her ankles rested on both sides of the tub, then her legs straddled him, pinned him to her and moved with a rhythm wild and furious until what was left of the water in the tub had turned cold.

That's what the pearl handle had meant to her. Now she was angry because, of necessity, it had to take a different meaning.

...if I'd had that razor on me, I wouldn't have called Cyrus. I'd have cut that motherfucka into...

She closed her eyes and imagined his flesh curling like pale thin ribbons around the moving blade.

Thinking of it, and of Tommy, caused her skin to grow hot and when she opened her eyes, she wondered again how long Cyrus had been talking and what had he spoken about. She nodded at polite intervals and continued to listen to her own voice.

Earlier, on the subway, she had tried to close her eyes but all she saw behind her lids were the dirty, reconditioned power machines and work tables piled high with blouses, pink, yellow, striped, checked, stacked to the ceiling. When Monday morning came, the blouses would there waiting, along with the rusted, antiquated fans that did not work and more noise than she could bear. And worse, the floor man had begun to look at her in a way she didn't like, as if it was her turn to make him happy.

But the minute he asked, she would be out of a job because she was ready to let him know that the price was twice as much as his wife charged.

*** ***

When she had stepped off the "A" train at 125th Street, it was a decision she had made without thinking. The Apollo's curtain was going up just as she bought her ticket.

She sat alone in the dark, un-self conscious among couples, and allowed Dinah Washington, in a magnificent white silk gown, to take her away to a time and place - she wasn't sure which – where the only sound more urgent than that powerful voice had been the press of her own tears.

At midnight, she walked up 8th Avenue, unmindful of the music spilling from the corner bars and the crowds moving around her. She sang to herself 'what a difference a day makes', testing the deep and easy inflections Dinah had used.

She detoured to 7th Avenue to pass by Smalls Paradise and the Red Rooster – two of Tommy's old haunts. She turned again at 145th street and walked past the Club Harlem where they had once danced. The air itself seemed musical, pushing in currents to move her along with others dressed for the week end. They flowed in and out of these streams, in and out of the music, the clubs, and the dance halls.

Rose watched them.

...They'll be coming to hear me too. All of these people. I will speak to Blue again. Matthew and his guys could back me. And Cyrus will be my manager. I'll try out at the Amateur Hour. I'm gonna do it, Tommy. And everybody'll be coming to hear me. I'll go on tours, make record, sign autographs...

The applause was ringing in her ears when she approached the corner and saw the familiar figure haunting the stoop. She was glad his back had been turned and she was glad that the phone in the Peacock - out of order half the time , and hogged by the number runner the rest of the time – had been working when she rushed in. And when Cyrus and Matthew entered, she had wanted to cry with gratitude.

*** ***

Cyrus stopped speaking and turned to face her. She had no idea what he had said or how she was expected to respond. It seemed like a good moment to take a sip from her glass.

"Cyrus, I'm glad you're looking out for me because I don't know what I'd do without you. I know I'm making things hard and complicated but I can't leave. I just can't."

She raised her hand to her face and absently brushed back her hair. "You don't understand, Cyrus, but I can't leave now. There's things I have to do and I'm gonna do it in spite of Rhino. Whatever's gonna happen, is just gotta happen."

There is a reason why I can't leave and I wish I could tell you. I wish I could tell you that Tommy is still in this place. His picture is on my dresser, smiling at me. Some of his clothes are hanging in the closet. The soap he used is in the bathroom. And his hair? Yes, his hair is still in one of my combs. And if I breathe deep enough I can almost catch the fragrance of his shaving stuff.

In the middle of the night, when it's real quiet, I close my eyes tight and think real hard , and I hear him. I hear him. He's still here. I am not leaving him.

Chapter Sixteen

RHINO

The heat was concentrated in the small room as if the window had been sealed and forgotten. The air was so sour, it smelled almost sweet.

The window in fact was wide open and the limp curtains, tied in a knot, moved only slightly in the faint breeze. Rhino paced in the small space then finally sat down on the edge of the narrow bed in the dark and stared at the gray patch of visible sky.

" Time to make a move. Time to make a move. Ain't nuthin' for me in this fuckin' place. Nuthin'. The Coast. I oughtta be hangin' on the coast with cats who know what the fuck they up to 'stead of comin' back here to this nowhere situation. To this shit. Ain't supposed to stand on the stoop 'cause Blue think he own it. Like he gonna charge me rent for standin' and then tryin' to finger me for his jam. Fuck him! And that bitch, that bitch comin' out that bar ...shakin' her ass like she own all the sidewalk. Put me in the can for two years for nuthin'. For nuthin'. Good thing Cyrus and Matthew was with her, I'd a...."

He heard Blue's laughter again. It filled the room and he could not move away from it. He looked around in the dark for something to throw, break, or press between his sweating palms. The mirror over the chest, destroyed earlier, hung in its frame like a silver spider web. He opened each drawer in the chest randomly, then slammed them shut, seven drawers, slamming each one harder than the last.

"Fuck her! Fuck 'em all."

He paused to catch his breath and felt the sweat run down the pit of his arms. A hard knot formed in his stomach and sweat soaked his shirt so that it was wet against his skin.

He dropped his pants to his knees.

"She see this, maybe she change her mind..."

His breath was loud and painful as he stood wide-legged in front of the window and stared up through the darkened court yard.

" ...lights out but she see me and she know what I got for her".

His back arched and his eyes bulged, and finally he doubled over and called her name as he fell back on the bed.

*** ***

Chapter Seventeen
THE VISIT

2.a.m.

Cyrus returned to his apartment, placed a stack of Billie Holiday records on the turntable and sat in the dark trying to hear something above the smooth despair floating through the room.

" … Now what? Rose heard not one word I was saying. I'm back to square one."

He thought of his life, her life, his promise and his failure to protect her, to get her to understand the danger she was facing and suddenly he felt he was drowning, pulled down to an unmeasurable depth by something unknown. He closed his eyes and imagined his life force bubbling out and floating dizzily to the surface in a thin phosphorescent strand. He struggled against the image and rose from the chair, needing air to catch his breath and a wide space in which to arrange his thoughts.

He switched on the light and glanced at the clock.

"…2.a.m. I wonder if – no, she's probably asleep. Or will think I'm crazy to come knocking on her door this time of night. No. better to head back down to the Alley. Matthew and Blue will want to know about Rose, and there'll probably be more sound and opinion and no decision."

A minute later, he wondered what he was doing when he rang Effie's bell. And a few minutes after that, when he heard the muffle of her slippers move quietly toward the door and stop, he held his breath. What could he say when she asked who was there?

And why was he there?

But it was too late to walk away. He closed his eyes, wondering how to tell her.

...I'm here because I don't feel like tasting another drop of bourbon on my tongue tonight. Because I need to think aloud away from the distraction of jazz and jokes and cigarette smoke. Because I need a cup of real coffee. Prepared slowly and carefully and maybe laced.. with concern. I'm here because...

Her eyes were glazed with sleep when she opened the door but grew large when she looked at him.

"Cyrus. What's wrong? Did something happen? Oh, I'm sorry. Don't stand out in the hall."

She stepped aside, tying her satin quilted robe tightly at the waist. "Come in. Come in."

He followed her down the long hall and in the living room watched as she clicked on the small table lamp near the sofa. She was not wearing the scarf and in the soft light her hair framed her face like a large and delicate halo.

"Come. Have a seat. You look tired, Cyrus."

She thought about the remark and quickly corrected herself. "But I suppose at 2 a.m. it's hard to look otherwise."

She laughed and he relaxed. She seemed not in the least angry or surprised at this odd-hour visit.

"I'll fix us some coffee," she murmured and disappeared into the kitchen.

He took a seat in the chair nearest the sofa and leaned back to look around him. The lamplight reminded him of the warm glow in the old private Pullman railroad cars, but the cast in this room was richer. There was life in this room.

For years, when he had listened to bar talk, barbershop talk, and the small talk of knowledgeable intellects when they occasionally dropped their masks, he had heard men speak with feeling and memory. Men able to describe a chance glimpse of a woman – dancing at a party, raising a spoon to her mouth in a restaurant, or simply handling oranges at an avenue fruit stand- and how that glimpse could somehow particularize her, and in the process move a man from curiosity to conversation, and beyond.

Now, sitting in the soft comfort of the room, listening to the woman moving about in the kitchen, he thought of his wife, Edna.

Years ago, when he had spied her in the school library on a gray Saturday afternoon, she had not said a word, had not even smiled when he dropped his books and clumsily tipped his hat. But in that glimpse, he had seen the sun in her eyes.

It had taken another week to actually meet her again and then she did not remember him. He apologized for not having made an impression. She had smiled and he went on to make up for the lapse. Memory unrolled like a dream. Less than a year of marriage too-good-to-be true before the epidemic had taken her along with two thousand other influenza victims and leaving him to walk down the aisle at graduation with only her picture pressed against him in his shirt pocket.

When he had gone south to find a job, he had also gone to find that private place in which to nurse his grief, but circumstance had turned him around, led him here, to this living room.

Now he needed to figure out, of all the women he had met- some serious, some not- what was it about the woman in the kitchen, with her halo hair and long legs and hint of hurt behind the set of her mouth when she smiled – what was it that had particularized her.

*** ***

In the kitchen, Effie watched the water percolate up the stem through the coffee, burst through the pot's glass bubble and drip down again to repeat the cycle. She lowered the flame and set about preparing a tray. She was wide awake now and wondered if the coffee's aroma or the thought of having Cyrus to talk to at such a strange hour had brought on the giddy feeling.

She glanced at the wall clock and decided that any hour would have been fine. There was so much she wanted to talk about and no one to talk to except Sara but the girl was still a girl and too young to absorb such things. Such talk would only have confused her.

But Cyrus was actually here and now her mind had gone blank. All she could focus on was his appearance.

...a three piece suit. At 2.a.m. Where in the world was he going? He could be home reading a book and still be dressed to kill.

Just like...that damn Maxwell.

She stopped in the middle of the kitchen as if to get her bearings.

What made me think that? A suit is nothing. Cloth. It's the body in it that mattered. Ah, but Maxwell had been sporting that sharp navy blue suit that night at the Savoy. Should've known something. Everybody roasting like ribs at a bar-be-que and there he was in all that heat, in that suit, leaning so cool against the bar.

And I never figured it out. All my friends saw it – or saw something – except me. Even Mavis – so cross eyed that half the time you couldn't tell what she was looking at, poor thing, -even she noticed.

'...look too damn formal to me,' she said. "Look like the kind who'd tip his hat and say please before jumping between your legs.'

She had laughed but shut up quick when she saw how quiet I had gotten. Maybe she couldn't see straight, but it was a whole lot better than not seeing at all.

The coffee pot nearly boiled over. She quickly removed it and emptied it into the silver server. The steam rose in her face and she closed her eyes and took a deep breath, luxuriating in the strong fragrance.

Beware.

...Of what? My own stupidity? Ah, but the Savoy nights was almost like a drug. I knew I was good looking and I knew Maxwell was watching so I showed off. Danced every dance while he just leaned back against the bar, hands jammed in that doubled breasted jacket and cigarette hanging so loose from the side of his mouth. Smoke made him squint like a gangster.

He watched me and I knew it so I showed off. Worked that Lindy, Charleston, Camel Walk, and the Sand. When 'Second Balcony Jump' came on, I was up again although my feet were killing me. Danced so much, my toes were like balloons ready to pop and afterward I could hardly tip home.

I showed off because he was so handsome and I was hoping he would ask me to dance. When he finally walked over, all he wanted to do was talk. Imagine. Politics at the Savoy. It was hard to be polite, one ear on him and the other on Lionel Hampton 'Flyin' Home'.

..If I had wanted politics, I would've gone around the corner to the Garvey meetings. I did listen – until I couldn't stand it any longer, then away I'd go again, out on the floor with a real sharp partner, feeling like I was some kind of star and knowing that Maxwell was watching. Who had time to think? I had come to dance and the beat was all I heard.

..But he waited and walked me home, week after week after week and that's how it started. He smiled and talked through the beat and I began to like what he said. I began to love his intelligence. That's how it started.

Beware.

Especially of handsome men wearing those damn sharp suits.

She arranged a plate of muffins on the tray as Cyrus called out.

"Effie, can I help you with anything?"

His voice was soft, sleepy, and she wondered if he sounded like that when he woke in the mornings.

"No. No. everything's ready, Cyrus. Be there in a minute."

She entered the living room and he leaned forward to clear away some books on the low table. She watched him, suddenly suspicious of his movements, his neat handling of the spoons and cups.

Beware.

She wanted to laugh and cry all at once.

He was reaching across the tray for the sugar bowl when he glanced at her, then slowly put the bowl down.

"I'm sorry," he whispered. "You know, I'm really sorry. I had no right to do this, to wake you at this hour. I..I.. can come back some other time."

He rose to leave and Effie, wondering when 'some other time' would ever come again, pushed the memory of suits and navy blue double breasted jackets and whatever else that was confusing to her – squeezed it into an unused corner of her mind and smiled. "You wouldn't have rung my bell," she whispered, "if something wasn't bothering you, Cyrus. I can see it in your face as plain as day. What is it? What's the matter?"

Out on the avenue, two floors below, an ambulance raced toward some unknown tragedy. The siren filled the living room and they remained silent, suspended for a moment by its thin sound. It filtered away as quickly as it had come, subsumed in the ordinary noise of traffic. Now, Effie listened to the light click of Cyrus's spoon against the rim of his cup. Then it was quiet again.

She gazed at him, wanting to reach through this silence and take his face in her hands and touch the small brown mole near his brow, then trace his narrow nose and his bottom lip which seemed so much fuller than the top. She wondered what he would say if she did that. Instead, she folded her hands in her lap. "What is it? Tell me."

Cyrus looked at her and then said, "it's nothing. Well, no. it's something pretty serious." He fell silent again, wondering how to begin to talk about Rhino without mentioning Rose. He wondered why Effie disliked Rose and why Rose hated Effie.

"Listen," he began again, searching for a neutral opening. "Did you know that the Morgans are planning to move? Because of Rhino?"

"I know. Sara told me. She's very upset. You know how she feels about Theo, but that's not what you want to talk about, is it?"

"No, that's only part of it, I suppose. The problem is that we all feel so – helpless. Rhino's presence is pulling this place apart but we can't do anything until he does something."

" –And by that time, I'll be too late," she whispered, finishing the thought for him. "It'll be after the fact."

She waited, watching him in the pause. She did not want to discuss Rhino, the Morgans, and least of all Rose, that damn whore of a niece.

But she wanted to talk in order to get certain things out of her way. He needed to know why the rich mahogany color had drained from her hair. She needed to push the fragments of her history directly into his path, like boulders, so there could be no skipping around them or mistaking them for other debris. She needed to know what he would think if she told him that her late husband-beloved, devoted, hardworking - all the adjectives women add to convince themselves that the man was worth sweating, fighting, maybe even dying for- was less, a whole lot less, then he seemed.

What would he say if I told him that some nights, Maxwell had come to bed with his pajamas buttoned to the neck over his underwear and breathed through unbrushed teeth in order to keep me on the far side of him. What would he say if I told him that he had never wanted children, yet had started calling me 'ma' on our wedding night and had never stopped.

What would he say if I described the reverend's late night summons to 'come fix the church lock, the church clock, the damn church bell, and the church's fucking phone, all of which seemed to break down exactly in the midnight hour one night a week every week like clock work, yet Maxwell was never able or willing to fix anything at home – including me.

Let me tell you all of this now, to get it out of my head and out of my way, our way, so that you can begin to move in my direction...

Ah, I want you to move toward me, Cyrus. Hold me. Touch me. Touch my face, my shoulders, and my mouth. Touch my breasts even though they never, ever, looked like Rose's. well, touch me and maybe...maybe they might...

She realized as she listened to his quiet voice, that if her history stayed inside her, it would remain in the way, unexamined, and she could only offer small comfort, and he could offer her none at all. She could allow him to open her robe- or she could open it herself – and feel him bury himself in her for the moment. But she needed not this middle of the night coming together but a clear idea of what lay ahead for both of them. Without this, she would be a temporary thing, a now thing, no past and no future and no better than that damn whore.

*** ***

Windows are never closed on Friday or Saturday nights, especially in summer. Too much is happening along the avenue.

Open windows allow night sounds to rise and drift like vapors into the dead air of lonely rooms.

Open windows allow witnesses, two, three, four flights up, to referee street fights and second guess love duels and traffic accidents.

And on quieter weekends, predict how far a drunk will bob and weave before the sidewalk comes up to greet him. The avenue is unrehearsed theatre, a dependable resource for shut-ins, gossips, wives of late working husbands and husbands with bored wives. Night noise is a lifeline for those facing life alone.

Some of this floated through Effie's open window. Strands of music from the bar, the screech of tires from a hailed cab, laughter strong and immediate, and all fading too soon to silence.

Cyrus placed his cup on the table and studied Effie's face in the soft light, wondering how to move beyond the inadequacy of small talk, open up to larger issues without her disconnecting from him.

"Effie, what…I need to know what.."

She did not hesitate. "I'm thinking of a lot of things, Cyrus, but you ask me. Ask me the question and you'll get an honest answer."

Her response surprised him. No puzzling over the question in order to turn it inside out. No time to mount a defense. And it did not fall, leap or rush from her to hang in the silence to make him wonder. It was a simple reply.

She leaned over to glance out of the window, then turned to face him. "Ask me and I will tell you but it may not be what you're prepared to hear."

"What you tell me now, Effie, will not change you. I mean, it will not change how I think of you or feel about you or…"

"How do you feel?"

He leaned forward, his hands on his knees, and he smiled.

"I feel as if I should've said hello to you years ago. Years ago. Not in a loving way, because you were a married woman but in a way to let you know that I saw something special.

"So what you tell me now, I'm ready to hear. I know you've been through a great deal. I went through it too, years ago. I think it's the price every one of us has to pay for-"

"For what?" she turned suddenly and pulled at her hair, hoping he had the answer. "What could be worth this?"

Her face was creased with agitation and Cyrus thought about it before he finally whispered, "intimacy, perhaps. And validation. We gamble, we risk everything when we enter a relationship. We gamble that the person we love will remain in our lives and that happiness will be part of the equation. We take on unknown factors. We enter a dark alley blindly, hoping that when we emerge at the other end, the person with whom we went in is the same person who comes out. Sometimes we're lucky. Sometimes, not. Sometimes we lose the person altogether in the passage and we come out alone, devastated, but with a hell of a lot more insight. We look back at that dark passage and wonder how we ever made it."

Effie nodded and the halo shimmered in the dim light. She held both hands to her head and closed her eyes. "I had trouble in that tunnel, Cyrus."

"I know."

"It almost killed me."

"I know, Effie, I know."

"What else do you know?" The question slipped out and she watched him expectantly.

"I don't know much more, Effie, except that you seemed.. not very happy. That you were trying to accommodate yourself to.. a situation. That's what I saw. Or thought I saw. But then, there are lots of couples living unhappily ever after and trying to accommodate themselves to any number of situations, mostly I suspect, because they feel they have no other options."

"What did you see in Maxwell?" she whispered, knowing that the time for telling had finally come and perhaps hearing her words spoken aloud, she might come to understand the why of it.

"Maxwell? Cyrus waved his hand. "Well, now, I'm not a fortune teller or one who reads life lines in an outstretched palm."

"Pretend you are. What did you see?"

"Well I couldn't figure out what I actually saw. It's like when someone happens on an accident. They're on the scene technically, but logically, it's hard to pinpoint certain details. Your husband was handsome, intelligent, an immaculate dresser but even as he spoke, he seemed to be playing to some unseen presence. His movements and manners were precise, careful, like an actor afraid of being caught without his stage makeup."

He leaned over and looked at her closely in the half light. "It was almost as if he – tell me, did your husband...did he...did he have an outside interest?"

Effie paused in the silence, wondering whether to laugh. The word 'husband' sounded foreign to her now. She wanted to laugh because it was she who had been the outside interest. How could things have gotten so mixed up? She wanted to howl at the very mention of his name and at her own blindness.

"Outside interest?" she repeated. "Yes, you might say that."

There was a silence again in which she wondered if she should excuse herself and leave the room, re-heat the coffee or get more cake, anything to give her a chance to catch her breath but she made no move. She felt tired. Her back and her knees ached.

Cyrus continued to gaze at her. "You know, sometimes a rational and otherwise intelligent person turns out to be the biggest fool – or as Blue would say- 'you just can't see for lookin'."

"What do you mean?"

"Just what I said. I should have said hello long ago."

She closed her eyes and bowed her head. "Oh, Cyrus, I – "

She had been sitting stiffly with the quilted robe-more suited for winter- wrapped tightly around her. She was accustomed to stretching out with shoes off so that her toes could move. Now she sat so straight, every joint seemed in rebellion and she felt the perspiration pour in a stream between her breasts.

"What is it?" His voice moved around her in the near dark. "What is it?"

'You won't believe this but I – my legs, my knees.."

"Oh."

Perhaps it was her knee. Perhaps not. Perhaps it was the unalterable feeling of isolation, the sense of sleeping, breathing, thinking, and being alone without the thin connecting thread of another's touch. Perhaps it was the turning over at midnight in a bed that had all the room in the world and waking in the morning to the solitary sound of the radio busy with pronouncements of weather and war. Perhaps it was the single place setting and lone bath towel.

Isolation settling in, solidifying like small stones between the joints and crippling the soul.

He took her hands and held them, then slid his fingers along the quilted robe and understood that it was really the weight rather than the warmth that she needed to feel against her skin.

"How long have your..legs been hurting?"

"It..it comes and goes," she murmured.

"Well, let's see…"

It was a simple matter for him to find a small basin in the bathroom, a jar of scented oil in the medicine cabinet, and a large bath towel.

He had taken off his jacket and rolled up his sleeves and she was surprised to see how well formed his shoulders and arms were.

"Let's see," he said again and started slowly, examining her toes, gently pressing and massaging one at a time. He brushed the pumice over her heels. He oiled her soles and ankles and then massaged her calves with a firm in and out rhythm.

She lay back and closed her eyes wanting, not wanting to believe the feeling that rose within her. A fine and light sensation that made her catch her breath until it hurt. Then floating away, dissolving into something more urgent.

She heard him whisper, "relax, relax, Effie, you're too tight. Just relax.."

"I can't. Oh, I'm not…used to this.."

"You will be, Baby. You will be. It just takes...time and we have all the time in the world.."

His hands moved, touching the soft part in the back of her knees, and then eased up along the inside of her thighs. He massaged her stomach and her hips, pressing lightly, before he moved down to touch her calve again.

"Ah, Baby, what beautiful legs. What long and beautiful.."

She helped remove his shirt and watched as his trousers slipped to the floor. The boxer shorts came off and he stood before her. She could think of nothing else as she came out of her robe. Nothing except the man before her, bending now to cup her breasts to his mouth. His breath was in her ear, his hand moving down on her stomach. Down.

The heat rose. Night noise faded and only the sound of him prevailed when she pressed him to her.

*** ***

Later, when they lay side by side, exhausted and full and empty and she inhaled the heavy scent of her own salty taste from his lips, that would be the time to curl into him and rest her leg on his smooth stomach and talk, time then to fill in the gaps he had only guessed at.

Chapter Eighteen
FOUR A.M..

4 A.M.

Blue leaned against the bar tapping his foot as Matthew came off a solo that brought the crowd to its feet. The place was busy for a Monday night, probably because word had gotten around that half of the musicians from 52nd street had decided to drop in for a session.

The set ended and Blue had a double Cutty Sark waiting when Matthew approached.

"Soundin' good, man. Held it all the way. All the way..."

Blue was proud of him and proud that the Alley had the talent to attract more talent. All the dollars in the world couldn't have brought these guys under one roof at the same time: Cozy Cole, Charlie Shavers, Buck Clayton, Coleman Hawkins. They were here, jamming for the hell of it.

And the crowd probably would have trampled Rhino if he had been anywhere near the stoop. But luckily, lately, he had been keeping his distance.

"So it was on the money?" Matthew asked, still sweating from the performance. It was like old times, old friends and big names, passing through The Apple on their way to or from France, Morocco, Japan.

It had been a cool casual coming together where the solo had each man poised, head to the side, ready at a fraction to slide into an improvisation that might not be heard ever again.

The air was thick as each came on to soft scattered applause, soft yet strong enough to let the man know that he knew what to do when the time came to do it.

Matthew knew it even though his shirt was wet and his legs were still unsteady from the encounter. Carving, the old timers called it.

"Damn," was all he could say. He laid his horn on the bar and picked up his glass. "Damn."

"Man, Cyrus should have popped in," Blue said. "He would've heard some rare stuff.."

"Well, the night's still young. He might still make it."

Blue glanced at Matthew but said nothing. He knew Matthew was excited and had lost all track of time. He did not have the heart to mention that in another hour, the sun would be up and an hour or so after that, most nine-to-fivers would be grabbing a bite to eat and heading for the subway, on their way to work or looking for work. They would not be coming into an after hours spot.

"Seems like Cyrus been makin' himself kind of scarce 'round these parts lately," Blue continued. "What's goin' on?"

"Nothing but the rent as far as I know," Matthew said, draining his glass.

Blue poured another round. "Think the heat got to him?"

Matthew glanced away and tried not to smile. "Your guess is as good as mine. And it depends on how you spelling the word these days."

"What word?"

"Heat."

Blue placed the bottle on the shelf and leaned against the counter. "Well, I'll be damn. It ain't who we think it is, is it?"

"Ask me no questions, I'll tell you no lies."

Blue tapped him lightly on the shoulder. "You aint no help at all. How you expect me to keep up with the latest if you ain't talkin'?"

"It ain't about playing mum. He ain't opened his mouth yet. Not one word. I just sort of put two and two together and guessed the rest and I may be wrong. I'm waiting for official notice, just like everybody else. When it comes to a man and his sweet thing, I say my name is Les and I ain't in that mess."

"Well, whatever your name is, they callin' you. Step on out there and show 'em what you made of."

He watched Matthew weave his way around the small tables. . There were about 150 people in the place. In the dim light, cigarettes glowed and an occasional match flared. Every table had a set up and standees lounged against the bar. On stage, Matthew raised his horn, closed his eyes, and low murmurs subsided as his notes flowed through the darkened room.

In another hour, Blue thought, Sandra would have to call Matthew's job and explain that her husband would not be coming in today, he was not feeling well. Blue sighed and put another case of beer on ice and unpacked another bag of paper cups.

Right now, Matthew was standing tall and feeling fine, doing what he lived to do. The long gray postal day was one thing, but these hours belonged to him.

He thought again of Cyrus and wondered if what Matthew hinted at was really true. And if it was, how come nobody saw it coming.

Chapter Nineteen

THERE ARE NO TRUE SECRETS.

A secret thing remains so only as long as the sharers acknowledge their investment. Even so, there is the subconscious urge to enlarge the circle of investors.

Or, the secret is betrayed by the investors themselves, in ways unknown to them: perhaps the smile of a woman, vague and soft, that speaks of dreams.

Or the barely perceptible light in the eyes of a man signifying a new-found and stunning satisfaction.

*** ***

When Effie and Rose met in the hallway, they went through the usual ritual dance of ignoring, sidestepping, and moving on quickly as if each had urgent business waiting around the bend of the stairs.

One day Effie caught Rose by surprise, bathing her with a glance that was almost lukewarm. Rose stared, unable to say a word, but listened as Effie continued on her way. The sound of her footsteps fell as delicately as a small girl's and Rose imagined she heard Effie singing under breath. She was *singing.*

Around that time, Rose began to wonder about Cyrus's preoccupied silences, long periods when she had had to repeat questions a child should have grasped at first hearing.

One week later, when she entered the lobby, Cyrus was on the stairs ahead of her. He did not see her but she spied the bunch of long stemmed roses cradled in his arm.

On the landing, she slowed down, stepped softly, and stopped altogether when she heard the jingle of keys. *Keys turning in a lock to an apartment that was not his own.*

She crept up the steps and listened to a muffled sound, a whisper of surprise from behind Effie's half closed door.

Rose closed her eyes and leaned against the banister. "No. This can't be. It can't."

One flight up, she put her key in her own door and slammed it hard enough to rattle the pictures on her wall. In the kitchen, she poured half a glass of Johnny Walker.

...Maybe I didn't see him. Maybe it was somebody else bringing that stuck up bitch those flowers. Maybe..

When she placed the empty glass in the sink, the vision, through her rage, was even clearer.

*** ***

Days later, Rose paced the floor in Cyrus's apartment. "How could you let this happen?"

"Let what happen?" he asked.

For the last week or so, he had tried to be patient and ignore Rose's small throwaway remarks but now an edge had crept into his voice. His niece was prying into something that was none of her business, and was presuming to chastise him in the process.

"Allow what to happen?" he repeated. "I asked you here because I wanted to discuss your voice problems."

"My voice problems?"

"Yes. When Miss Adele called, I was surprised. She's the best in the business and since I agreed to pay for your training, she called me. Wants to know why you've suddenly lost your enthusiasm. You know she handles only dedicated singers. If a person shows no promise, she shows them the door. What's happening with you?"

Miss Adele, a Julliard graduate, taught voice technique and it was true. She didn't waste her time or the student's money. It was inconceivable, Rose thought, that Miss Adele would take the time to call Cyrus.

Rose had started her lessons only recently and in that short period, had already felt a difference in her breathing. She did not have to cut a note so quickly and the tension in her neck had all but disappeared.

But Miss Adele said nothing about a lack of concentration. Instead, she had called Cyrus. Had actually taken the time. It had never been a question of money as far as Miss Adele was concerned. She had performed in Europe for years and had returned home to Harlem with three trunks full of furs and a small chest filled with so much jewelry, it would have taken a year to wear the same diamond twice.

It was not a matter of money. Rose glanced at Cyrus now and had to be careful how she answered.

"I haven't lost my enthusiasm, Cyrus. I just got ...side-tracked."

...Side-tracked by something that's none of your business, Cyrus thought, but he let a minute pass before he answered.

"Your voice should be your first order of concern. Nothing else matters at this point in your life. You can't afford to get side-tracked."

Rose knew he was right and this made her angrier.

"Is that why you didn't mention anything? Because you didn't want me to get...side-tracked?" She had stopped in the middle of the room and faced him.

Cyrus was sitting with his legs crossed, his right ankle propped on his left knee. He uncrossed them and rose to his feet. When he spoke, his voice was even enough to mask his rising anger.

"My dear girl, let's understand where we're heading in this discussion. I'm your uncle, not your son. I have an idea what's bothering you and I think we should at least be honest about it. You're angry because of Effie."

"What about her?"

"You're angry because I'm keeping company with her."

Rose remained silent although a thousand different responses churned inside her.

...So he's finally admitted it. Keeping company. He's probably doing more than that. But how could he, as smart as he is, fall for that woman.

He's no fool. What did she do to pull the wool over his eyes? What did she say? Her husband is dead only a year, and she already has another man crawling into her bed. And Cyrus of all people. How did this happen? How come I didn't see it sooner? I could have warned him. Let him know what a sneak she is. So damn prim and proper, staring down her nose at me and all the time had her fish hook dangling in deep water. That skinny bitch!

She was angry simply imagining the two of them together, laughing and perhaps sipping tea – old people were good at tea-sipping and telling old jokes – and beyond that? Had Effie actually gotten him into bed? Effie, with her old woman's white hair and long skirts who was now tripping down the stairs like some damn young girl?

The thought made her dizzy.

She turned to stare out the window, hoping to control her agitation. Across the avenue, the neon sign over the bar was not yet lighted and the sun illuminated the gray outlines of the huge bird. Even without the flashing lights, the Peacock's plume was imposing. It spread over the entrance like an invitation and Rose concentrated on the double doors, watching their rhythm as they swung open.

She wondered about the people moving in and out and about the unspoken feelings masked by too many doubles and too-loud laughter. The juke box endlessly spilling the same tune from its Christmas tree ring of light. And in a corner at the end of the bar, a voice dry as chalk humming along, struggling between sips to keep at bay the reason why he was there in the first place.

And although she tried hard not to think of it, there came to the back of her throat, the memory of the tart smoothness of Dom Perignon. It came in a rush and she put her hands to her mouth to keep from crying out.

Dom Perignon. Dom Perignon. And Tommy's fractured image gazing at her in the mirror as she raised the tulip shaped glass to her mouth. That back room. How large would the stage have been, and what kind of lighting would Tommy have put in to highlight her face? Her records would have been on the jukebox.

She pulled her attention back into the room where Cyrus was waiting. She wanted to let him know the feeling that gnawed at her. And her fear that too many things were slipping beyond her. People she loved and trusted and whom she had expected to be there for her were being stolen away. Her center was disappearing and she felt adrift in a sea of helplessness.

...I can't tell him. I'm afraid and alone and I can't find the words to tell him. My own uncle...

"You know, Rose," Cyrus continued, "Each of us is given a gift. And I don't have to tell you that what we do with it, largely determines our happiness, our lives."

Rose said nothing, wondering what gift Effie possessed.

...Whatever it is, must be damn near priceless. Cyrus has never in his life looked so damned... satisfied. That woman's gift, whatever the hell it is, should be patented.

"Miss Adele mentioned that a voice like yours comes along only once in a great while," he said. He shook his head and in the silence, Rose understood.

She had been told more than once that the low notes were beautiful and haunting. She did not say that that was the only language she knew, that she could not express herself any other way, and that there had been times when those sounds which came from somewhere so deep inside, surprised even her.

She moved from the window. "I have to go. Miss Adele has a thing about punctuality. We can finish this talk later."

Cyrus watched her open the door. He could have asked what more they had to discuss, but instead he said, " Give my regards to Miss Adele."

*** ***

Rose strolled up 8th Avenue toward the Dunbar Apartments. She moved through the Saturday afternoon crowds and gazed at the stoop loungers, waved at those she knew, and wondered if any of those smiling faces had had to cope with an uncle who, despite his intelligence, was stupid enough to fall in love in his old age.

Chapter Twenty
APT2B

The room held an odor of old shoes. The stained, gray, bed sheets were thrown back across the iron headboard and the pillows were piled on the windowsill.

The seven drawer chest was the only other furniture in the room, the chair having been removed to avoid the pile of clothing which never found its way onto the hangers in the closet.

With the chair gone, the clothes were thrown on the floor. Rhino leaned on the chest and looked into the splintered mirror.

I know it's hot. So what. That ain't no fuckin' news .I got to take a bath? I'm okay the way I am. Matter a fact, I'm fine. And I'm grown. Got some damn nerve tellin' me when I gotta git in the tub. She don't like it, let her hold her nose. Hold her fuckin ' breath until she drop dead. What I care.

Just took a rinse, let's see, last week. Now, what more she want? Room smell? Bed smell? I don't smell nuthin '... must her imaginin' again. I don't smell nuthin'. I ain't gittin' in no water, not til I'm damn good and ready and I ain't ready.

He moved about the small room in a tight circle, kicking at the clothing on the floor, then stopped once more to peer in the mirror.

I'll throw some more a this lotion on, then I'll be alright. I'll be straight. Don't need her to tell me what I gotta do.

His arms and neck were sticky with the lotion and he picked up a tee shirt from the pile on the floor and wiped the excess off.

I'm straight. Let her say somethin'. She can't say nuthin'.

He put the tee shirt on and turned the lock in the bedroom door.

Gotta git outta here, take care a some business and see about…Damn! Fuckin' shirt stickin' like glue..

Place mighty quiet, damn quiet. What she doin' in her room. Doors locked, fans goin' in every window. All that electricity. Must be in love with Con Edison to use all that juice.

Get on my fuckin' nerves. 'Do this. Do that. I ain't doin' shit.

When I do, I'm a be ready to split. This damn shirt is stickin' to me…

It's rainin'. Ain't this a bitch. Hoooo…Rain ain't never stopped no show.

He slammed the door extra hard so that at least one picture on the wall would fall off and Fannie Dillard would know that he had stepped out, that he had business to take care of and didn't need to waste time hanging around listening to her.

Chapter Twenty One
CONFRONTATION

August rain, when it finally comes, makes up for days when the heat rebounds from the pavement in visible waves; it makes up for times when there had been a run on colas, melons, ice cream and ice, and nights when families spread blankets on roof tops and fire escapes and slept with their mouths open to the stars.

The first drops were a fine negligible sprinkle quickly absorbed in the accumulated, iron gray street dust. Then the zig zag flash lit the sky and people turned off radios and moved away from any task that required electricity, leaving it for another day. Thunder followed, sending children running as a thick wet curtain descended.

Sara stood on the top landing looking out on the wet roof. She had cut short her visit to the library in order to meet Theo and speak to him for at least five minutes.

Her mother had finally calmed down and allowed him to visit-not long visits-but visits nevertheless for which she was grateful. But there was never the privacy she needed in order to say the things she wanted to say. Most of the short time was taken up with questions her parents asked: school, school, and more school.

And Theo patiently, or impatiently - depending on how he felt about the questions- tried to answer.

Her mother and father looked on these visits as the most hazardous development in her young life and made no move to leave the living room when he rang the doorbell.

She always sat near him, but there was not a chance of touching his hand. She could only glance down at his fingers, breathe in the light scent of his cologne, and wondered how long he intended to visit – come calling – as her mother like to say- under such circumstances. …

Perhaps he's already tired. Ah, if I could only see him.

She leaned against the door frame and watched the downpour. The sky was tinged deep purple and huge electrical forks lit up the surrounding clouds but the wet wind was cool against her skin and she remained on the landing.

"He's not coming. Probably thinks I'm already in the house because of the rain. Or maybe he simply isn't coming..

She turned to retrace her steps and stopped.

Rhino was standing in front of her.

"I seen you," he whispered by way of introduction. "You new here."

She could not speak. She had glimpsed him from a distance several times and Theo had warned her to give him a wide berth.

"He's crazy, you know. He's a killer."

She stood still now, paralyzed. There was no room to give him a wide berth because he was easing up to the top step, one hand on the banister and the other on the wall, blocking her way.

His face resembled a bleached skull, brought into sharp relief with each flash of light. She backed away from the face as much as from the sour odor that filled the landing.

"So where you goin', baby? Can't run nowhere. It ain't good to be up here. This is my spot. My spot, and it ain't good to-"

She opened her mouth to scream , to yell at him or anyone who would hear her, but the rain drummed against the roof and beat against the hall window and no one heard as he propelled himself forward and grabbed the front of her blouse.

"No!! Nooo…let me alone! Let me – Somebody, help me!

Help meee !!

They fell against the wall as he tried to tear at her skirt. She hit his face and his head with the book and kicked at him but it was useless. He was so close. His breath made her sick.

"Get a..way! Get away from me… Help!!"

"My spot, bitch! You hear me. You just like that other – "

When she fell to the floor trying to curl into a ball, she thought she had lost her mind, thought she saw two pairs of feet, four legs, then sounds, heavy, grunting, and out of breath. And through a fog of fear, she heard Theo:

Rhino, I'm a whip your ass!!"

Theo's fist came down in an overhead arc that knocked Rhino against the wall. More blows to the chest and stomach caused him to collapse to his knees.

"I wasn't doin' nuthin ! The bitch started it!"

Theo jerked him up and held him arm's length and hit him again, then again, knocking off his glasses, and again until blood spurted and covered both of them.

"You put your hands on her. You put your hands on her. You-"

Theo closed in. His fists moved like a boxer's against a punching bag fast and deliberate, keeping the rhythm with a low choked monotone. "You. Put. Your-"

Again and again and again until he finally felt his own breathing about to give way. He ended by pushing Rhino down the flight of stairs.

Rhino lay for an instant, then scrambled to his knees and crawled away.

Theo and Sara stared at each other. She was shaking and her teeth chattered out of control. She looked at his bloody shirt and opened her mouth and could only manage to form a silent O. She shook her head and could not call his name.

"I should've killed him," Theo finally whispered, trying to catch his breath. "I can't believe he did this. I should've- "

"What…what…what?"

He looked at her tear streaked face and loose hair. Her blouse had come out of her skirt and he knelt to put one of her shoes back on her feet.

"Next time I see him, that's what I'm gonna do. He won't get away with this."

She could not answer but allowed him to lead her down the stairs. She heard him say, "My mom's home. She'll know what to do. Don't cry, Sara. Don't cry.."

Her head rested on his shoulder, and she never felt the steps under her feet. She was too frightened to care if anyone saw her and too confused to explain.

*** ***

When Theo opened the door, Sandra was preparing the table for dinner. She looked up and the plates fell from her hand.

"Oh my god! My god!!"

Mathew heard the clatter and came running. "What happened?? What -?"

"Rhino caught Sara in the hall. Coming up the stairs," Theo said before Sara could speak. "He tried to drag her to the roof but I caught 'im."

He led Sara to a chair. "I caught him," he repeated, amazed at his capacity for invention. No point in making a bad situation worse by saying she was up there all alone, waiting, where she had no business.

"We had a fight and I whipped his – I whipped him good," he stammered.

Matthew stared at his son's bloody shirt, and then closed his eyes. When he opened them again, he went to the kitchen drawer where he kept his tools, pulled out a claw hammer and headed for the door.

"Matthew, wait!! Where are you going?"

"To finish the job, Baby. The shit done hit. That motherfucker has got to go!"

"Wait, wait!"

" That's all we been doin', the whole damn house, we ain't been doin' nuthin' and look what happened. Look at Theo. Look at that girl, shakin' so bad she can't even speak. They both coulda been layin' up there dead. Goddammit, look at 'em!"

He moved toward the door and Sandra rushed to stop him. "Wait! Matthew, please, please. Let the police-"

"No! He'll be long gone by the time the cops decide to come."

Sara leaned forward suddenly and put her hands to her ears. The sound she made, a cry less than a whisper, stopped them all.

Theo put his arms around her shoulders. "It's gonna be all right, Sara. It's gonna be all right."

Matthew and Sandra exchanged glances as the girl turned in the chair and clasped her arms around Theo's waist. She buried her face in his bloodied shirt and could not stop crying.

"..Theo. Don't leave me...please...don't leave me..."

"I won't, Sara. I won't."

Matthew's mouth fell open as he watched his son smooth the girl's hair from her face. He had never seen such an expression of unspoken love. In that gesture, his young son disappeared and Matthew watched a young man – a carbon of himself- emerge.

"I won't leave you," the young man whispered again.

It was as if the two of them were alone in the room.

Sandra watched also and could not believe what she was seeing. The pity she initially felt for Sara dissolved in a blinding flash of jealousy, fear, and finally, rage.

...My son could have been killed – was willing to be killed – for this girl, this little nobody who slipped into this house from some damn, nameless place, crept into our lives and disrupted everything. She has turned my son's head so much, he was willing to lay his life on the line for her. For her.

She felt something rise in her chest and cut her breath off. What had also frightened her, although she could not name it, was the current of barely contained sexual tension. She saw it in Sara's tight embrace, heard it her son's husky voice, smelled it in their stained and bloody clothing. The sight and sound engulfed her and everything in the room seemed to spin.

"Matthew. Matthew, I.. Oh – "

"Sandy, hey. Take it easy. Here, sit down, Baby. It's gonna be all right."

He didn't know what to do next: see about Theo with all that blood on him. Call Sara's folks. Call the police. See about Sandra. Or go and find Rhino and kill him so that none of this would never happen again.

"Theo, go change that shirt. And soak your hands in some ice water. They'll be twice their size in an hour. Come on, Sandy, you gotta lay down 'till I get back."

"Please, Matthew – "

"I'm takin' Sara home."

He still held the claw hammer and they stared at it in silence.

"It's comin' with me," he said. "Just in case."

Chapter Twenty Two

THE READING

The storm that everyone had prayed for, passed so quickly, it was as if it had never happened.

The next day dawned with temperatures already in the seventies and the gray pavements once again baked in a combination of dust and heat.

By noon, the Bradhurst Avenue pool was filled to capacity and the senior lifeguards ordered the two story high wrought iron gates closed. Those who were turned away headed for the Odeon or Roosevelt theatres where, for twenty five cents, they could sit through the double feature, three action chapters, the Pathe newsreel, the Sepia News, two coming attractions and a half dozen cartoons in air conditioned comfort.

Those with a little extra change, stopped first at the Trelawny West Indian Bakery on 8th Avenue and took their lunch with them.

Clothilde and Stanley ignored this heat as they returned from the doctor with Sara, grateful that their daughter had not been seriously injured. They entered the lobby and Clothilde paused.

"Listen, Sara. There's soup on the stove. Fix your daddy a bowl and take some yourself. Then I want you to lie down. I'll cook a big meal when I get back."

"Where you goin?" asked Stan. He leaned against the metal banister, his anxiety visible on his drawn face.

"Where I told you," Clothilde replied softly, touching his shoulder. "Shouldn't take but an hour."

She left the house, crossed 8th Avenue, and entered the small shop next door to Connie's Pool Room. The space was dark and cool and Clothilde breathed in the heavy scent of eucalyptus but the past 24 hours had been too much and the knot in her chest did not loosen.

MissLady, as Clothilde called the tea reader because she had never learned to properly pronounce her foreign-sounding name, opened the lace curtains and sighed.

"I heard what happened, Clothilde. Please come on in," and led Clothilde past the long counter filled with painted statues, incense burners, oils, and candles to the familiar glass topped table in the rear of the store.

An hour later, Clothilde opened her purse, untied a small handkerchief and counted out ten one dollar bills; money pinched and saved by doing without stockings, hairdressers, and movies. Money accumulated by substituting something she liked for something less whenever she shopped.

She especially missed the movies because of the free dinner-ware on Tuesdays. She had managed to collect one complete set, gold rim with floral pattern, and only needed the teapot to complete a second set which she hoped to give to Sara.

She was proud of herself. No matter how tight things got, she always stuck by her mother's advice: "Earn a dollar, save a dime."

She bit her lip now as she counted.

This money had been put away to buy a surprise gift and maybe a fancy dinner when Sara graduated. She was also going to buy her a new dress from a proper store. When her daughter got ready for college, home sewn dresses would be a thing of the past. Clothilde imagined Sara in something fashioned of silk, an elegant garment befitting her new station.

Clothilde's fingers were wet with perspiration as she placed the bills one by one on the table and tried to control her fear. If she cried again, her vision would blur and she'd have to start all over.

MissLady gathered the bills carefully, and placed a small package in Clothilde's hand.

"Listen my dear, you follow these instructions and the situation will right itself. No need to move away. He will smell your fear and like the dog he is, he will come after you. But you do as I advise and he will not return to the house you are in."

She paused before adding. "If he does, he will not walk out alive."

Clothilde stared, her fear so palpable, she stammered when she opened her mouth. The reading said nothing about dying. She closed her eyes. A minute passed before she was able to speak. "He will not come out alive? Are you certain?"

Clothilde had on several occasions visited MissLady although she knew without being told that her future was largely what she made it. There would be some detours but she was on the right track. She knew this. The times when she had come to have MissLady examine her palm or read the leaves in the bottom of her cup had been times when Stan had dragged home too tired to eat, had crawled into bed without bathing, and later had cried in his sleep cursing the lawyer and flailing the air with his scarred fists, frightening her.

Would they ever see the end of this dark and dangerous path? Would her husband ever have the chance to relax. Breathe. Smile.

At those times she needed to hear the sound of her affirmations shaped in a voice other than her own so that she could absorb the spiritual inflections and repeat them in a whisper near Stan's ear as he drifted off to sleep.

But right now she needed something stronger and more decisive.

"I know of that young man," MissLady continued. "He's lost and angry and looking for something he will never find in his present state. He is carrying an old injury and he will violate everyone and everything in his path. In the end, it is this anger that will undo him. Right now, he is the one running and hiding. There is no need for you to do so."

Clothilde nodded. *I can manage this. I know I can.*

MissLady emptied a small vial of rose water on the table and wiped it away with a linen cloth. Then she blew out the candle and removed her indigo head wrap. The meeting had ended and she walked Clothilde to the door. She was small and thin and her face was unlined and Clothilde often wondered about her age but there was never enough time to figure it out. She nodded, held the package in her hands and stepped out the door.

Clothilde moved across the avenue and entered the house as if she were in waking dream.

We don't need to move. Now what? Ah, look at my troubles this day, ah Lord, look at my troubles.

He will not come out alive. He will not –

Stan opened the door and put his finger to his lips "She's asleep. Let's sit in the kitchen."

"So how much it cost for all this?" he whispered as Clothilde emptied the package on the table. He gazed at the assortment of candles, powders, incense, Dead Sea salts, and strips of parchment paper and never thought he would be resorting to the ways of his grandmother and mother. He thought he had left all that behind when he signed his name to that contract.

(MEN WANTED TO PICK FRUIT. GOOD MONEY. SUPPORT YOUR FAMILY IN STYLE WHEN YOU RETURN.)

...if we return, he and at least a dozen others had thought as they waited on the crowded pier.

The freighter had been small and ragged and the contract workers held no illusions. Many of their relatives, friends, and others they had only heard about, had died of dysentery, pneumonia, and the snake bites that had gone untreated by the field bosses who were only interested in filling the day's quota.

Some men had fallen for the American prostitutes and robbed of what little they had earned. Others had returned with T.B. and other conditions untreatable by the local remedies.

Stan had no illusions. In fact, on the boat, he had been so tight-lipped, the others had nodded and called him, 'Stan, the man with the plan' and he had smiled faintly.

Yes man, is for me to know and you to find out.

And the first night after a day in the blistering Florida fields, he had left the barracks and eased away on feet swollen with fatigue and insect bites and with the fruit pulp sticky on his aching fingers.

Then came the hard walk through strange towns, long days and odd jobs, insulting pay, no pay, work in exchange for a meal; and days of hard, hard hunger before he reached New York only to sit doubled over, dizzy from cramps and thirst, on a Harlem park bench.

A short fat man walking a Doberman stopped and tapped him on the shoulder. "Wek up, boy. You mekin' we place look shabby. Wha' wrong wid you?"

And no need to hear his story, the familiar accent had been enough for his lands-man to help him out with a meal, a shower, some hand-me- down clothes, and point him in the direction of a low paying, no questions asked, back breaking garment center job which seemed, at the time, like a gift from heaven.

*** ***

Sitting at the table watching his wife empty the package, he wondered if he had come full circle. He had wanted to kill the man who had touched his child, kill him and run with his family back to the safety and familiar poverty of the small island he never should have left.

Last night, Clothilde had needed all her strength to talk him out of it.

"You'll have blood on your hands, Stan. The authorities will hunt us down like dogs. You want to die in prison and leave this child fatherless? Eh? Answer me that?"

He had not known what to say. The initial shock had been so great, seeing his daughter so frightened and disheveled, he had burst into tears. Then he had grabbed the knife and was out the door before Matthew could hold him back.

In the hallway, Cyrus and Rose had both opened their doors to the noise and rushed to help Matthew.

"Be cool, man," Matthew had said as they struggled to bring Stan back into the apartment. "Besides, the cat ain't even in the house no more. He's long gone. I wish I could catch up with him myself."

"Ah'm gonna kill him on sight!" Stan had shouted.

*** ***

Long after the others had left them alone with their sorrow, and Sara had fallen asleep from exhaustion, Clothilde hugged Stan to her until the shaking subsided. Then she started talking, and talked because that was what she knew how to do and she did not finish until dawn.

"Listen, Stan. Listen to me. She's still our little girl. She will be all right but we must give it time. We mustn't make matters worse for her. Try to understand this. If it hadn't been for Theo- oh, what a wonderful boy. I knew it from the beginning."

"But suppose the boy hadn't come up the stairs at that time," Stan said. "What then? What would've happened?"

It was five a.m. and they had spoken in whispers so as not to disturb Sara in the next room. Clothilde had sat on the edge of their bed, quiet. Then, she leaned close to him and murmured, "God was with Sara then. God sent that boy to look after her at the right time. Now, even though we can't go to the police, we gonna take care of things."

"How?"

Clothilde had risen from the bed to stand by the window. She leaned against the window sill and watched the dawn inch its way up the deserted avenue. Every bone and muscle in her ached. When she turned to face her husband, her frame was silhouetted against the fading arc of the street lights. Her fine features were shadowed and her voice was softer than usual.

"There's more than one way to skin a cat, she whispered.

Clothilde lit the incense and waited for the thin spiral to send its fragrance into the air. Then she lit the candle and held the small square of parchment with the one-line message over the flame. Stan found himself closing his eyes again and inhaling the scent of sandlewood. The familiar fragrance burned his nostrils. His eyes remained closed as he listened to the murmured incantations.

Chapter Twenty Three

APT 2B

Sandra refused the glass of lemonade Fannie Dillard offered and remained standing in the doorway of the kitchen.

"..You know what happened, don't you?"

"Yes, Sandra, I do. Babe told me when I went to get the newspaper. Everyone on the avenue is talking about it, warning me that Richard had better not try anything with Theo."

"Where is Rhi- where is Richard now?" Sandra asked.

"Honest, I have no idea. That boy rushed in here last night soaked in blood - even his glasses were bloody. He snatched the money that was on my dresser and left. Didn't say a word. Just ran out."

Fannie sat at the kitchen table, her hands absently smoothing invisible wrinkles in the linen cloth. Her hair was gathered in a loose bun at the nape of her neck and her yellow cotton blouse showed damp circles under her arms. A minute passed before she spoke again: "You know, Sandra, people are supposed to feel joy in their children. But I don't know what happened. I feel like my whole life just passed me by. I can't remember one good day in the last twenty-some years, not one."

She glanced up with a look of complete bewilderment. "First my child, then my grandchild. I don't understand.."

Her voice died away and she continued to smooth the linen cloth. Sandra remained silent. She still had not taken a seat.

"You know," Fannie continued, "my pressure is so high, sometimes I see double."

"What?? Fannie, are you taking anything for it? Any medicine?"

"No. I mean sometimes I remember but I have too much other stuff on my mind and I..I..just don't know. Sometimes I forget."

Sandra was surprised that she spoke of this condition so off-handedly, especially of the signs she seemed to ignore because she was too busy worrying about someone else.

Fannie put her hands to her face and Sandra thought she was about to cry, but she said," you and Matthew count your blessings. You have a wonderful boy. A nice young man."

Her voice trailed away leaving Sandra to wonder if she really knew where Rhino was and whether she was protecting him to the last. After all, everybody in the whole house, it seemed, was after him. It was only a question of who would reach him first.

A nice boy. A wonderful boy. My son would have been a dead boy if he hadn't known how to defend himself. Now two of his fingers are broken. We don't know if he'll ever play an instrument again.

"-And you're sure you don't know where he's gone?"

"Please, Sandra. I'm not hiding or protecting him. I'm tired of doing that. I haven't heard a word from him since last night, not even a phone call."

She rose from the table. Come. Let me show you something."

Sandra followed her down the long narrow hall, through a large and immaculate living room, and opened the door to a small bedroom.

The odor made Sandra step back and she turned away from the sight of the clothing piled on the filthy bed. She was embarrassed for Fannie because they both knew this room did not belong in this apartment.

"When I get my strength back, I'll clean this up," Fannie whispered. "I know he won't be coming back any time soon."

"I suppose not," Sandra murmured, backing further away. She glanced around the living room with its beige, camel-back sofa, the polished oak coffee table and the silk- shaded lamps with the marble bases which must have cost a pretty penny when Fannie had been working. But her blood pressure had affected her vision, forcing her to retire early from her garment center job. Sandra knew that Fannie's check stretched only so far. How could Rhino take what little she had?

"Well, Fannie, you let me know if you hear anything."

She paused at the door and then added. “And let me know if you need anything from the store, okay?”

Fannie nodded as Sandra opened the door, trying not to hurry.

Chapter Twenty Four

APT2A

Sandra watched Theo polish the clarinet for the third time in as many days.

"Theo, you know the doctor said to take it easy with your hands."

"I know.. I know.."

She watched him hold the instrument at different angles as if he had used it in his recent battle and was now inspecting it for signs of damage.

"Everything will be all right, Theo. I know it will. The x-rays.."

"I know, Ma. I know."

He placed the clarinet in its case. The index and middle fingers of his left hand bandaged together in a splint made movement awkward.

"Is it okay if I go to the movies?"

She looked at him and wanted to pray again. Her tall, handsome, sixteen year old – nearly a man – asking permission. A few days ago, before all of this happened, he would have said, 'Ma, I'm going' and she would have said, 'you know what time to be in'. And that would have been that. She wanted to cry because she could never again be satisfied with just that. Now, every move required a serious session of questions and more answers.

"Which movie?"

"The Odeon. Me and Jimmy and Tight and Dexter wanna catch the two o'clock-"

"You mean, 'Jimmy and Tight and Dexter and I" she patiently corrected him.

"Yes, we'll be back around six."

"Need any money?"

"Nah. Pop already gave me yesterday."

She watched him walk toward the door and wanted to call out 'be careful, be careful, be careful. Please, please, please.

But he was with his boys, not Sara. Nothing would happen.

*** ***

She put on a pot of coffee and waited for the aroma to wake Matthew. Five minutes later, he wandered into the kitchen. His pajama bottom was draped around his hips and his chest was bare.

"Sure is bright in here," he said and kissed her good morning although it was already after 12 o'clock.

"The sun is no brighter than usual. Go brush that whiskey off your teeth. You want scrambled or sunny-side up?"

"Neither. How about hard boiled?"

"You giving me a hard time?"

"No, Baby, you know I'm kidding. Any way you want to fix 'em is all right with me. Where's Theo?"

"Up and gone like most people who know the value of time and know better than to waste it sleeping."

"I know, but where is he?"

"Went to the movies with his boys. The Odeon. He'll be back by six."

"How's his hand looking?"

"He's worried. Maybe you should talk to him when he comes in."

She put the toast, bacon, orange juice, and scrambled eggs on the table. Her ritual of saying grace before meals had enlarged into a prayer for protection. She had whispered this quickly before Matthew emerged from the bathroom, and then said the regular, abbreviated, grace aloud with him.

"Amen," he said quickly, reaching for the coffee.

She enjoyed watching him eat but felt a pang of conscience. "I didn't mean to wake you so early, but Theo was going out and I wanted somebody to talk to."

"Somebody to talk to – you could've gotten on the phone and called the weather report."

"I thought about it but they can't talk back…"

"Neither can I, half the time."

She reached across the small table and pressed her hand lightly against his unshaven face. "I love you, Baby."

"I love you,too." He winked and added, "almost as much as I love these eggs. Damn if they ain't good enough to eat."

Matthew smiled as his wife closed her eyes. Seventeen years of marriage and she was still quiet about the things they did, and enjoyed, in the middle of the night. He was even more surprised that things had picked up quite a bit since the incident with Rhino.

She's afraid, afraid for the kid, afraid for me. When we makin' it, she forgets about all this, but then we finish and everything comes right back..

He gazed at her and wished he could make the forgetfulness last just a bit longer. He wondered how a man-any man- could condition himself to go fifteen rounds in a championship fight and yet was only able to go one or two rounds in a bed. It didn't seem fair.

She raised her cup again and he watched her.

She hasn't said a word about moving though, thank God..

"You know, it sure was a surprise to find out that the Morgans don't have their papers," he said.

"I knew something was wrong the minute they knocked on the door the other night and said they wanted to talk," Sandra murmured. "Imagine asking us not to go to the police, that they would take care of everything themselves. They're so hard up, how can they take care of anything? And poor Clothilde, such a sweet woman, so dignified but so soft and helpless. If we make a complaint, Sara will have to go to court along with Theo. What a mess. The poor woman doesn't know which way to turn."

"I know one thing," Matthew said. "The word is out. That's all they talked about last night in the Alley. If Rhino's seen, he's gonna wish he wasn't. I heard that even Babe got some money out on him."

"Wouldn't surprise me if she had had money out on him as soon as she heard he was back," Sandra said.

She could barely swallow her coffee. She did not mention that she had paid a visit to Fannie Dillard two days ago. Nor did she mention that she had seen Clothilde entering that root-woman's shop near Connie's Pool Hall the day after it happened.

*** ***

That day, Sandra had been in Brandi's Beauty Spot, sitting in the chair near the window and able to see everything.

Brandi had been complaining about the characters on 'As The World Turns' and Sandra only half listened. She was thinking about the characters in the real life soap opera unfolding in 1048.

Theo's hand is broken. Sara was nearly raped. From the way she looked, Rhino probably would have thrown her out the window if he could have. Now he's nowhere to be found. His grandmother is scared witless and so is Rose. Even Effie seems different somehow. She's looking and acting so strange. I don't know. Not strange but more alive, for some reason. And Matthew says the business in the Alley has kind of fallen off and Blue doesn't know what he wants to do about it. Says Tommy had that chance to kill Rhino and didn't do it.

Brandi suddenly pointed the hot curling iron toward the window. "Well, looka there. Ain't that the west Indian woman whose daughter got raped?"

"She was not raped," Sandra answered quickly, knowing how a rumor can take on a life of its own. She watched Clothilde move like an old woman across the avenue. "The girl was not raped," she said again. My son got there before anything happened and he beat Rhino to a pulp."

"No kiddin'! Well, good for Theo. Good for him." Brandi said, waving the hot curling iron much too close to Sandra's forehead. "Rhino got what he deserved and more's coming, I can tell you that. I mean that root-woman is serious. Heard when she gets mad, she gives a discount. Now me, I got me some good numbers from her. How you think I opened this shop? Told me to put my last ten dollars on 252 and damn if it didn't come out the very next day. Straight. I kissed that factory – coulda been a pie factory for all I cared- kissed that sucker goodbye and been doin' all right ever since. I can say one thing for that woman: 'you can't lose with the stuff she use.' "

She placed the iron back in its rack and angled the scissors to clip Sandra's hair. "Girl, it's good thing there's a full moon tonight. Your ends is split bad. Sure sign of nerves. Your nerves is bad. I'm gonna give you these clippings. Take 'em home and burn it in a brown paper bag.

"And you know who else I'd like to get in this chair?" Brandi went on, clucking her teeth impatiently, not waiting for an answer. "That Effie, pour soul. If I could snatch that woman in here and get hold of that mop, I'd have her lookin' like sixteen again in fifteen minutes. Imagine waltzin' 'round with all that white hair like it's in style or somethin'."

Sandra remained quiet, listening to the click of the scissors near her ear. She glanced at the wall clock near the oval shaped *LETS-BE-FRIENDS-DON'T-ASK-FOR-CREDIT* sign and wondered what was taking Clothilde so long. She had entered that store nearly an hour ago.

"She's been in there a long time," Sandra finally said.

"Naw," Brandi smiled, "that ain't no time at all depending on the problem. Me, I was in there for three hours and I figured it was probably an hour for each digit, seemed like, but it was worth it. Don't worry about her. She'll be all right when she come out, I guarantee it."

When Clothilde emerged, Brandi and Sandra leaned forward, pressing against the plants in the window to get a better look and to speculate on the contents of the package Clothilde held away from her chest.

"Must be some serious stuff. Look how she's holdin' it. Like something's gonna jump out there and bite her," Brandi whispered.

They watched her move across the avenue as if she were in a trance.

"Well, Brandi sighed, "I wouldn't want to be on the receiving end of that gift, whatever it is.."

She nodded and removed the plastic cape from Sandra's shoulders. "No sir, not in a million years."

*** ***

That had been two days ago.

Sandra thought of Brandi now as she sat at the table watching Matthew help himself to a second serving of bacon and toast. It occurred to her that she never did burn the clippings. She must remember to do it today, before it was too late.

Too late? She didn't know if there was a time limit or why the bits of hair had to be burned at all. She would do it. Perhaps it would change her luck. Theo had not mentioned the girl's name lately but in unguarded moments, when he sat in the window facing the courtyard, even though he was not able to play, his expression said enough.

*** ***

She looked up and caught Matthew's gaze. "What's the matter? Need your coffee warmed up?"

He placed his cup on the saucer and nodded. "No, Baby. It's not the coffee that needs heating."

"What is it?"

He reached across the table and took her hand. "I see you kinda tightening up. How about me sliding your fine frame into a warm bubble bath and after, I'll give you a special massage."

"Ah, Matthew."

"Head to toe," he murmured, moving to stand in back of her. "Just the way you like it."

Before she could answer, he smiled, "Baby, don't look at the clock. We got the whole day. The whole day."

She felt his fingers in her hair and she rose to lean against him. His skin was wet.

"Ah, Matt. Matt."

"I'm here, Baby."

He touched the sash of her robe and she forgot about the clippings and the brown paper bag.

Chapter Twenty Five

THE PARK

Colonial Park

A week later, the phone call that Fannie Dillard had been expecting finally came. She murmured a short reply, placed the receiver in its cradle and waited until nightfall before she left the house.

She moved through the traffic of 8th Avenue with the heavy shopping bag, hoping no one would offer to help her.

She saw that the Peacock was filled with the usual middle-of-the-week crowd taking advantage of the after work two-for-one special. It was nearly 8 o'clock and the other shops nearby were closing.

..Thank God. Not too many folks I know.

She hurried past the stores and headed toward Bradhurst Avenue only to find the benches surrounding Colonial Park still crowded from the afternoon and children still playing on the swings and sliding board.

Onlookers congregated around the checker players under the street lights. A hoarse voice called a bet on the black queen. Dog walkers strolled in the evening heat. She skirted past them and wandered through the tennis and volley ball courts where the nets had been removed for the night.

Beyond this, the band shell where the Monday night dances were once held loomed gray and empty and the large semi-circle dance space was deserted. She sat down on a stone bench near the perimeter, wondering who would hear her if she had to scream for help.

Despite the darkness, she could make out the narrow concrete steps near the band shell that led down to the equipment room under the stage.

That's where he is. I know it. Oh, God. The boy didn't do anything but go from bad to worse.

In the distance, the playground sounds rose with an occasional cry louder than the rest and she strained toward the voices.

Children. Able to laugh and play like children.

A few feet away, a cloud of insects nicked and pecked at the dim lamplight, then eventually found her. They were the summer-night, low flying kind, which under ordinary circumstances, would have sent her running, but now they merely annoyed her. She brushed at them without thinking, listening for some other sound, unsure of what it would be.

When she heard it and turned to see her grandson approach, her heart contracted and she caught her breath at the sight of him.

In the dark, layered with dirt and dried blood, his skin resembled the residue of a fire not quite extinguished. She could not make out his eyes behind his glasses and so waited until he spoke.

"You got what I asked for?"

"Yes, including the bus ticket, she murmured, trying not to stare. His clothing was torn and dirtier than she had imagined.

"Here," she said, handing him the bag. "Here's a change of clothing. I'm glad you made up your mind to leave. It's the best thing. Too many people looking for you. Maybe you can come back in a year or so- when things kind of quiet down. Right now, it's not good."

"You told me all that on the phone," he said, reaching into the bag. He did ask how she was feeling, but rummaged beneath the clothing and pulled out the container of food.

Fannie watched him eat, quickly and noisily, dropping the chicken bones where he stood. He scooped up the rice and greens with his fingers and ignored the juice spilling down his arms.

"You ain't bring nuthin' to drink?"

"The bag was heavy enough, Richard. What with the clothes and all. Isn't there a water fountain somewhere around?"

"I'm sick a water. That's all I been drinkin'. Nuthin' but water!!"

"Well, you'll have a chance to drink whatever you want in California."

"What's that supposed to mean?"

" Nothing more than what you want it to mean," Fannie whispered distinctly.

He looked at her, threw the empty container to the ground, and turned toward the steps. "You be hearin' from me," he growled. "Everybody be hearin' from me."

He was leaving. Walking away from her. She watched in the dim light, wondering what to do. Perhaps she would not ever see him again. Suddenly, she rushed after him, needing him to leave her with a word, a thought, one final look that would sum up or break down this whole experience.

One word that would explain to her how in the end he came to be hiding like an animal in a park where children laughed not fifty feet away.

"Richard. Why did you have to go and bother that girl?"

Fannie fought through her tears, trying one last time to understand. "She didn't do anything to you."

"How do you know?? How do you know she ain't done nuthin' to me," he said, wheeling around to face her. "You think you know so much, you all alike. You don't know shit!"

"Boy, you watch what comes out of your mouth. Watch what you say and how you say it. You may have killed a man but I'm still your grandmother - ."

"Ah, but you ain't my mama, now are you?? Answer me that, goddammit!"

She stood still. This hard language which he had never directed at her although she had heard him curse and cry in his sleep, struck her with the force of a hammer.

She raised her arms but before she could move forward-perhaps to embrace him or perhaps strike him back- she didn't know which- he had moved away and quickly plunged into the dense growth that formed the semi-circle of blooms around the stage.

"Richard!!" She called after him. "It didn't have to be this way!"

She called again and her voice came back to her in the dark. He had disappeared. She sat down again and squeezed her eyes shut.

In the silence, playground laughter drifted on the night air.

Chapter Twenty Six

TAR BEACH

1 A.M.

These are what you call the dog days," Blue said, folding his arms on the counter.

"And dog nights too," Matthew said. "Even the air conditioner has quit. Never seen heat like this."

It was mid-week and the band was off but Matthew was there anyway, listening to the jukebox. Blue uncapped two bottles of Rhinegold and pushed one across the counter toward him. "When I lock up, I'm heading straight for Tar Beach. "

"Gonna catch your shut-eye under the stars?"

"Yep. Lay in the cut 'til the sun come up."

Matthew nodded. "Tried it a couple of times but Sandy didn't go for it. Complained for a week about her back."

"Well, that's one of the hazards of married life," Blue smiled. "Cat can't camp out when he want to ."

At 3 a.m. there were two customers in the place, a short round man dressed in Bermuda shorts, striped socks, and a faded yellow straw hat. His face was wet with perspiration as he hugged his dancing partner, a thin woman half a head taller with a full bosom barely contained in a red halter blouse.

They glided slowly in the center of the dim lit dance floor and he gazed up into her eyes as it they had met only five minutes earlier. "In the still of the night" by the Five Satins drifted from the juke box and the couple moved to the beat, oblivious of the heat and the empty tables.

Blue glanced at his watch and stifled a yawn. Matthew had left two hours ago and no one else had come in.

Time to wrap this up. Cash register on zero. Love birds ready to dance into the middle of next week. Well, they got ten minutes. Cat oughtta be able to make his play. Glidin' and slidin' all night and the chick ain't heard a peep outta him. Strong, silent type. Heh. Well ten more and they glidin' out.Take it on over to the Moonlight Motel and hope the girl can understand body language. …

Ordinarily, he would be ready to stay open till dawn but tonight, because of the broken air conditioner, he felt drained. He remained standing, leaning against the bar. The Platters had come on and he tapped his foot to the beat in an effort to remain awake.

Finally the man spoke. "Okay Blue. See you later."

"My pleasure. Y'all come again," Blue said, quickly escorting them to the door.

A half hour later, he was on the roof spreading his blanket near the circle of chairs. There was no breeze. The residue of heat radiated from the tar and it felt soft when he lay down. He crossed his arms behind his head and allowed the silence to enfold him.

Up here, he had time and space in which to think. Time to gaze up at the galaxy and wonder, as he often did, what exactly was he doing with his life. Was he to run the Alley forever? Or find a nice girl, give up the night life and get married. Maybe have kids and retire to a farm somewhere?

He shook his head, losing the thought. Retirement to another place was not possible. He grew up here right on the block. His family had moved into 1048 when he was two years old.

And he would never give up the Alley. He had been the one who'd cleaned up the basement next to the furnace room for his poker games. Then he'd brought in that jukebox, a second hand model, big and flashy, where the selections lit up in orange neon when the buttons were pressed and the sounds of the Drifters, Big Mama Thornton, and Johnny Ace moved the folks from the small tables to the even smaller circle in the center of the room.

He had enlarged the space, constructing the dance floor himself, and polishing the hardwood board by board. The bar, the stage, and the jazz, seemed to follow naturally and he'd quit his dead-end day job to handle it all.

The deal with the landlord had allowed him to buy the seven-family building for five percent down and ten percent of the rental income mailed to the realty company for the following ten years. He owned it now free and clear and took care of the repairs although he still arranged for the rent to be mailed to a management company. That way he avoided any hard feelings that might surface from mixing business with friendship.

Life was good. Marriage was a good idea also if the right woman came along.

...something to think about. I'm almost 36. I want to be able to play ball with my kids before I'm fifty.

There was no moon. The few stars visible seemed close enough to touch. They appeared to float in a sea of ink and he was overcome with the pleasant, familiar feeling of drifting in infinite space. In the stillness, the smoke and whiskey and laughter of the Alley faded and he closed his eyes.

The small scraping sound woke him.

He turned over, resentful that someone else, trying to escape the heat, was about to intrude on his solitude.

He propped himself on one elbow, listening, wondering why the sound had not come from the stairwell.

The light metallic tapping grew louder and he knew that someone was moving up the fire escape. Blue rolled over and maneuvered within the circle of chairs on his hand and knees, cursing himself for not having brought his pistol or knife. He didn't even have his flashlight.

Last week, someone had gotten robbed while asleep in the park. Were thieves getting bolder? Prowling roofs now? No place was safe and he wondered what the world was coming to.

Well, whoever it is – a sneak thief probably- we just gonna have to duke it out. Shit. But.what if he's King Kong's daddy? Go toe to toe and I'm over the side, grabbin' air.

He scanned the area beyond the chairs hoping that someone had left an empty bottle or something.

But as usual, the roof had been swept clean after the poker game: no bottles, no cans, not even an empty paper bag had been left under the table.

He crouched on one knee like a quarterback and stared at the shaking handle bars of the fire escape.

The scraping sound stopped, then began again.

In the dark, he felt his muscles tighten.

" Fuck it. This is my turf. Whoever it is, ain't gonna leave here walkin'."

He crept toward the edge but did not look over. Instead, he cupped his hands to his mouth and the sound, a sharp piercing howl of a prairie dog, or more like a werewolf railing against a red moon, emerged, surprising him.

The handle bars shook and Blue heard the heavy sound of something falling. The handle bars shook again but the vibration was weaker. He leaned over the edge but could see nothing.

Maybe they busted into somebody's pad.

Then he made out a faint movement. Someone was moving fast down the fire escape, then dropped to the ground as soundlessly as a cat and disappeared.

Damn! Who the hell was it?

He returned to the circle to retrieve his blanket. His solitude had been invaded and his night was over.

In the hall, he listened to the echo of his footsteps. The lobby was empty. He moved past the row of mail boxes and stepped out into the street to scan the length of the block. It was empty also.

Across the avenue, a small mound of litter drifted in the breeze near the darkened Peacock. He scanned the block again, then moved inside, back to the closed heat of his apartment to sit by the window where solitude was punctuated by the hum and glare of the few passing busses. He heard the distant echo of footsteps and wondered who they belonged to.

Who was on the fire escape? What were they up to? Oh, shit!! Maybe...

He was on his feet, moving toward the phone. His fingers were unsteady and he had to dial Rose's number twice before he heard the ring. No answer. He slammed the phone down and tried again.

This time, her voice, drawling with sleep, came on.

"Who…hello? Hello?"

"It's me! Blue! You okay?"

"What? Of course I'm okay!!"

"I ..uhh..was lookin' for Cyrus because – "

"Don't you know where to find him? He's my uncle, not my son!"

Blue was left with a pain in his ear when she slammed the phone down.

.. Well maybe it wasn't who I thought it was. And at least Rose is alright. For now.

*** ***

When he woke, he ignored the sour taste in his mouth and reached for the phone again. The call was brief and his voice was low. His man at the three-two was equally brief: One note answers and they hung up.

Blue checked his watch and looked to the other business of the day: Soak in the tub, figure out his numbers, order more cups, whiskey, chasers, and then drink some coffee to hold him until he could make his way to Miss Laura's Luncheonette for the breakfast special. Today, Wednesday, meant broiled chicken livers, scrambled eggs, grits, and buttermilk biscuits.

In the tub, he closed his eyes, not to sleep but to think.

All that talk about not rattin' out Rhino. Don't tell the cops. He ain't comin' back. It was all bullshit. Everybody said he left for good, but who knows? Maybe it was him last night trying' to score. Maybe it wasn't. If somebody hadda called in on his ass from the jump, there wouldn't be no guessin' games now.

Well let's see what my man can do. Been payin' him since I opened the Alley. For years. Man made enough off me to build a damn Long Island mansion. Now he better look into this shit and tell me something. Make sure Rhino's long gone. Piss or get off the pot. Otherwise, I'll have to pull out my book and drop somethin' on him too.

The bath water had grown cold. Blue looked at the small clock on the hamper and reached for the towel. In front of the full length mirror, he appraised the figure staring back. Nearly six feet, dark, even features, clean shaven head, broad shoulders, muscled arms, and good teeth.

Well, ain't too bad. Could probably stand to flatten the stomach a little, maybe cut back on some of that beer. That'll do it. Otherwise...

He glanced at the clock again. "Oh, man! Got to make a move to Miss Laura's before all the grits get gone.

Chapter Twenty Seven

THE VISIT

Tar Beach socials were cancelled due to the heat. In open windows, large fans sang like noisy birds and every stoop on the shady side of the street became the primary property of the professional loungers.

The spot was crowded when a gray Chevy with dented fenders and dusted license plate pulled up in front of 1048. The watchers watched, recognizing a decoy even before the driver opened the door. No one living north of 110th street would dream of allowing a car – a man's pride, joy, badge of achievement, and lifetime payments- to reach such a low state. A good man's car was always washed, waxed, and ready to roll, even it only rolled from one curb to other for lack of gas money.

The watchers adjusted their masks and waited. The visitor, red faced in the heat, slammed the car door, glanced around as if to fix a landmark, then strolled purposefully into the building, as if he lived there – or owned it.

The watchers inched to the side permitting passage without touching and did not turn to help him scan the rows of scarred mailboxes.

He didn't ask what they knew and so they allowed him to search until he found what he was looking for and head for the stairs.

They knew Rhino hadn't been around since that thing with the Morgan girl. Time of that last big storm.

From the corner of their eyes, they watched the detective disappear up the stairs, then they opened bets on the time of his probable return. Two minutes or ten, depending on how snappy Fannie Dillard was feeling when he knocked on her door.

*** ***

Two flights up, Fannie Dillard took her time responding to the sound of the bell. Few people visited anymore and those who did, limited their talk; mostly to the numbers and the weather. Sometimes they discussed politics, with vague and neutral complaints about Mayor Wagner and how the current crop of local leaders weren't doing shit for the Negro community. And Fannie sighing, noted that the old leaders, a couple hundred years earlier, 'didn't do shit neither.'

In the small, vacant pauses, she drew a breath, waiting for the visitor to fill the silence with something else.

"So what you think about this weather?"

And depending on her mood, sometimes she nodded, not from irritation but from fatigue knowing that this visitor, despite the awkwardness, had probably meant well. But some wore on her nerves. When asked about the weather, she replied, 'that's in God's hands. All we can do is pray." And she looked them in the eye because she understood the real question and was more than tired of not answering.

"All we can do is pray", she repeated.

The weather, oppressive as it was, couldn't be changed but the political situation was different. There was the possibility of another uprising but she kept a lock on that thought. To mention it would be too likely to prolong the visit.

So there was mutual head nodding and a shift back to the safety of the numbers.

"Well, gotta go. Get that last digit in. What you dream lately? Ching Chow ain't told me nuthin' I can put a quarter on."

Fannie had also read the Daily News and counted the buttons on the cartoon character's jacket. Six were buttoned and one was unfastened. Today his picture was way back on page 60. "Here", she said reaching into her apron pocket. "Put sixty cents on the night track for me. 601 combination."

And she concluded the visit, pleasantly surprised that it had lasted more than fifteen minutes.

*** ***

Fannie now opened the door, looked at the stranger and placed herself in the entrance.

"I'm from the three-two," the man said, flashing his shield.

"Yes?"

She did not move but stood perfectly straight, the feeling of fatigue replaced by a rush of giddiness that seemed to push up and through her open mouth. Her grandson was gone, out on the coast living a new life.

"You looking for somebody?"

"Yeah. A man by the name of Richard- "

Fannie cut him off. "-he's not here."

She wanted to smile, something she had not been able to do in weeks. She looked at the detective's seersucker suit softened by sweat. He was tall and thin, and though his manner said he'd had years on the job, he appeared no older than thirty. She gazed at his reddened face and imagined if he had come under different circumstances, she would have invited him in for a glass of lemonade.

But she knew that he and others like him, given the slightest pretext, or no pretext at all, could hunt her boy down like a dog, corner and kill him and then walk away, wondering what all the fuss was about. Every other week, the tally in the Amsterdam News grew and she had had to stop reading it.

Now this man of the law was standing before her asking these silly questions, and she knew he carried as standard equipment, the 'extra' weapon that was always found 'not far from the suspect'.

" –So you haven't heard from him?"

"I haven't spoken to him in a while."

"You know he's supposed to report to his P.O. once a month and inform him if he moves."

"I didn't say he moved. I said I haven't spoken to him. When he's in, I'm out. When he's out, I'm in."

In the pause, Fannie Dillard knew when to lift her shoulders and smile wide – cloak the message so that she appeared as helpless as he wanted to believe she was. She watched him reach into his pocket and the tired feeling returned, nearly smothering her.

If he had a warrant, he should've said so in the first place. All this damn small talk for nuthin'.

He extended his card. "Okay. So how's he looking these days?"

"Looking? Same as ever," Fannie said, wondering where this was leading.

"So, he's okay?"

"He's fine as far as I can see.."

The man shrugged and Fannie tried to read his face.

"Well, okay," he said again. Tell him to call me. It's important."

She took the card and watched him descend the stairs. He took one step at a time as if he were thinking of more questions to ask and might turn back.

She closed the door and after a respectful minute and without glancing at the card, tore it into fine confetti and dropped in the toilet.

*** ***

Chapter Twenty Eight

APT 3B

One flight up, Stan eased the door shut and stood behind it, not daring to turn the rusty lock. He pressed his forehead against the wood frame and shivered as the sweat moved down the back of his shirt. When he finally turned away, he held to the wall as he walked.

In the kitchen, Clothilde looked up. "Eh? Stan? What's wrong? What is it, honey?"

She clasped her hands, and then moved to embrace him. "Eh, you look like you run into a jumbee, a ghost. All your blood fly from your face."

It was a few seconds before he could speak.

"The law was here. Snoopin'. I heard 'im – a white man- askin'after somebody."

Clothilde watched Stan lean over the table , his hands grasping the edge. When he moved, she saw the tremor.

"Maybe the man was lookin' for somebody else," she whispered. "Maybe for that Rhino."

He said nothing and she could look no further than at his drawn face, at the deep and indelible map work of fatigue and fear. She wanted to close her eyes and pray. And then rush to the bedroom and light another candle but the lines of the face before her told her everything.

"Sit down, honey. I'll make you some tea," she said quietly. "And we'll think what to do."

She felt the tight web pull within her chest as she moved to the stove and she wondered if she had the strength to turn on the jet or place the cups on the table. She said nothing because she could not trust the sound of her voice.

What went wrong? I followed MissLady's advice carefully. Never talked to a soul about it. Except to Stan. Maybe I wasn't supposed to say nuthin ' to him neither. But he's my husband. Why not tell him? Or maybe I shoulda kept quiet all together. Maybe..

She placed the kettle on the stove and glanced out of the window. On 8th Avenue, traffic moved. People moved. Two women waited at the bus stop . One had a fan that fluttered without effect. As slow as the cars and people moved, they were all going places too fast.

She thought of the way things were back home: evenings sitting on the narrow veranda in front of the house, the usual gathering place after dinner. She remembered the creaking of her mother's chair, safe and steady, rocking not quite in rhythm with the distant wash of the sea. Dark and soundless evenings in which little was said and less was expected. Only the hum of cicadas filled the silence after Radio Rediffusion signed off for the night.

But she had felt her restlessness even then, wanting many times to lift up her arms to push back the too-quiet, motionless, darkness. She remembered opening her mouth in a wide groaning yawn and her mother saying: 'proper girls don't make that sort of music.'

And she had closed her mouth and herself against the night and allowed large bright lights, floating lights, blinking lights, to come into her dreams. Lights brighter than anything she or anyone sitting there on the veranda could imagine.

And she had struggled to come out and away from that motionless darkness- to here, where headlights, street lights, stop lights, search lights – were as bright as she had dreamed but which also had the power to blind and confuse. To destroy the vision if one stared too closely or too long.

She wondered how to reach back into that long ago silence, the ancient nothingness she had complained of, reach back and wrap that darkness around her family like a cloak.

Across the avenue, the two women had not moved. The bus was taking its time. The fan holder said something and the other woman nodded, and both opened their mouths to small soundless laughter. Clothilde watched them, annoyed that she could not have been a part of it. When would she be able to laugh.

The whistle of the kettle crowded the room and the noise made her head ache. Below the sound, she barely made out her husband's voice.:

"No ifs, ands, or buts about it.", he said. "We leavin' this place."

Clothilde filled the cups and sat near him.

"What's the use we stayin'," he continued. "Always guessin' and second guessin', jumpin' and wonderin' what's gonna happen next. This is nuthin' but trouble. Even if the authorities lookin' only for Rhino, sooner or later they gonna get around to knockin' on this door. We have no papers, no card, no nothing but promises from a lawyer who's movin' slower than syrup. Better to find another place. Quick."

He dropped another cube of sugar into the steaming cup and stirred absently. "We'll do it piece by piece," he whispered. "Move a little at a time so as not to raise any suspicion."

"No," Clothilde shook her head. "This house is too small and too close for any secrets. Everybody knows everybody's business. They can't help it. Something happen on a Monday, the talk fly up like a bird and the news is old by Wednesday . I say we let the van pull up once and done.."

Stan looked at her. "If everybody knows everybody's business, how come we can't get a lead on Rhino? Where is he hidin' out? How come nobody's seen him, not even the police. He's probably in some dark basement by day and comin' out by night, like a suequant, thirsty for blood. And could be right around the corner for all we know.."

He drained his cup and rose from the table. "This weekend, we start packin '. By next week, we should find something maybe in Brooklyn. I hear tell it's pretty nice there. People mind their own business. But Sara is not to tell anyone."

He turned to face his wife. "She is to tell no one, you understand? Not even Theo."

Clothilde nodded. "Yes. Not even Theo. 'Cause if one knows, all will know." Even as she agreed, she knew a struggle loomed.

There would have to be a compromise. Perhaps Theo could meet Sara at school, or in the library, or...

Her head began to hurt again.

If they had had proper papers, they would have been able to relax, to stand up, but now they must run. Like thieves in the night. This was not what she had wanted for her child. She had dreamed of a proper education, a steady courtship, an engagement with a real diamond, then marriage, a solid, happy, prosperous marriage for her child.

And Theo had saved Sara's life. He was meant for her. He was ambitious, going to be like that man, Thurgood Marshall, who opened up all the schools in America for the colored children.

There must be a way. There must be a way.

Stan left the kitchen and she heard the creak of the mattress as he settled himself across the bed.

She knew he was not going to sleep but would be staring at the ceiling, thinking of this latest disaster. Ordinarily, she would have gone to him, let him lay his head in her lap and smooth his forehead until sleep, however fitful, came.

Instead, she remained at the table and poured another cup of tea. In the silence, her mind shifted like a kaleidoscope, with plots and devices falling in and out of place.

Chapter Twenty Nine

MIDNIGHT

"You ain't nuthin' but a hound dawg!!"

From the jukebox, Big Mama Thornton's graveled voice broke in a wave over the smoky dance floor and more dancers found a way to squeeze in to the already crowded space.

Blue checked his watch. The band should be coming off their break. The door opened and he looked up expecting to see Matthew returning from his usual walk. Instead, Cyrus strolled in.

"Well, damn. We was just about to give up on you," Blue smiled, pulling a bottle of bourbon from the shelf.

The door opened again and Matthew eased through the crowd. He spotted Cyrus and moved toward the bar.

"Hey, man. We were about to declare you missing in action."

"Premature," Cyrus answered against Big Mama's throaty wail. "Way premature. Don't order the flowers just yet."

"You all right?"

"Never felt better."

Blue and Matthew exchanged glances as Cyrus smiled. "I'm fine. Don't I look it?"

"You sure do, but- "

Cyrus winked at Matthew and raised his hand again. "Two fingers on the rocks and let Matthew have a double Cutty."

"Here you go." Blue said and watched as Cyrus raised his glass in a half toast.

"So what's going on?"

Blue glanced at Cyrus and rested his elbows on the counter. "You dropped in right on time. Was gonna wait till I got both of you together to pull your coat."

Matthew had raised his glass but now put it down."What's going on?"

"Well, I'm not too sure," Blue said. "Remember a few nights ago when I was gonna catch a nod on Tar Beach? Well, I was up there, but so was somebody else."

"That's not surprising in this heat," Cyrus replied. "Who was it?"

"That's just it. I ain't too sure. Usually my eye don't lie. But it was so dark I couldn't see two feet in front of me. Too dark for a positive eye dee. All I know is that somebody easin' up a fire escape after midnight usually ain't on legit business and I wasn't sittin' still for that. And from the side of the building he was operatin' on, I think it might have been Rhino."

"What??" Cyrus put his drink down.

"Yep. Your niece's window is on that side and I think it might've been him tryin' to creep her crib. Anyway, like I say, I might've been wrong about who it was but I let out a yell and the cat faded.

I ran down downstairs, scouted the street, but it was clean. I came back inside and hit the phone, called Rose, just to be on the safe side. Woke her up. And boy, was she mad, but she was okay."

The excitement of the evening, the music and the dancing, and talking to Cryus again, had drained from Blue.

"Got somebody working it," he said, keeping his voice low. "My man at the three-two will pick him up. If it was him, they'll let him know he ain't supposed to be light footin' no fire escapes after midnight. Don't give a damn how hot it is."

Matthew stirred his glass but still did not drink. "I thought he was long gone. Now he's back? Can't your man keep him out of here?"

"Not likely. Short of knocking him off. This is, you know, his legal address."

"Ain't this some shit. A killer with legal rights!"

"That's what I say too. But ain't nobody got a legal right to peep nobody's crib," Blue whispered, "so if it was him, don't sweat it. Somethin's gonna happen real soon ."

Cyrus raised his glass again. “Damn, I have to think about this. We’re not even sure it was Rhino.” “Maybe. Maybe not,” Matthew said. He pushed his glass back on the counter and made his way to the stage, shaking his head.

Cyrus watched him move through the crowd.

I’ll speak to Rose in the morning. If it was Rhino, and he’s that desperate, she’s in more trouble than I thought.

Chapter Thirty

APT 3A

The key turned in the lock and Effie rose from the sofa in the darkened room.

"Effie? You awake?"

She listened to his footsteps move down the hall, softly, so as not to waken her if he thought she was asleep. Some nights, she would be sleeping and then wake at his touch in the dark. She would turn to lie on her back, and listen as he undressed and ease into bed beside her. After the first kiss, she would fold into the curve of him, wordless, hungry, and the rest of the night was a wide awake dream.

Tonight, she stood near the sofa in the dark, waiting.

"Effie?"

The click of the light switch bathed the room and his eyes went wide at the sight of her. He stared open mouthed at her dark brown hair, cut shoulder length. The sides were swept back from her face and the curls held in place by a red elastic head band.

"What?? Effie, what - what did you - ?"

"Cy. I wanted to surprise you. I went to Brandi and asked her to _"

She sat down on the sofa and closed her eyes "Ah, I thought you would like it. I wanted so much for you to- "

He saw her agitation and moved to sit beside her. "Effie. Effie, listen . it's fine. It really is. It –it's just that it caught me by surprise and I wasn't.."

He didn't know what to say. First the news about Rhino being back in the house, and now this. The night was too damn full of surprises.

"You don't like it," she whispered.

"I, well, I-"

"I can see the look on your face. You don't like it."

He drew a breath and gazed at her in the soft light. He looked at her brown shoulders and the thin straps of the pink nightgown. Her feet were bare and the gown curled against her like spun silk. He wanted to touch her, lift her up and carry her to the bedroom where..where what?"

Memory unspooled like a reel of film, each frame so clear he ached to step inside, to feel again what he had felt all those other nights.

She is on him, moving in the dark. He could hear her breath, feel her skin, and her hair is a silver cloud floating down, drawing near, close enough for him to reach up and hold to her until his arms ached from the effort and she had drawn everything out of him.

Some nights he held her so close, tasted her kisses so hard, his mouth hurt in the morning.

"You're disappointed," she whispered. She leaned her head on his shoulder. "I saw it in your eyes."

"Effie, I'm not disappointed, just surprised, that's all. Just surprised. You can never disappoint me. Baby, I love you. And would love you if you dyed your hair green or cut it all off. You'd still be you."

He heard the small sounds and knew she was crying, knew she did not believe him.

"I wanted to be like I was before," she whispered. "I wanted to look like I used to look."

He closed his arms around her. "Effie, are you happy? I mean are you happy with me?"

She pulled away and looked up to face him. Her eyes were large and luminous and for a minute, she was silent. Finally she whispered, "I love you. And I want to make you happy. You know, when I looked in a mirror or caught a glimpse in a window, I was always reminded of – different things. I was blinded by what I saw. I lost sight of what was.."

Cyrus held her, listening to her breathing and he thought of scars – deep, psychic wounds not visible to the naked eye. But he knew that once the heart opened up, the wound would heal. He knew and would have to work at it.

"Effie, listen. You make me feel like the luckiest man in the world, and when we're together, not just in that bed together, but anywhere, I look at you, see your smile, and I feel ten feet tall."

She closed her eyes again and he watched her and wondered about dreams and how they sometimes bore no relation to reality, how reality itself was an illusion. The silver halo was gone, lost. Maybe the key to the dream was not to wake up. Keep it going. Forever, if possible.

Her hair would take some getting used to. He would have to practice a little and smile a lot. Learn to touch it the same as before, with the same soft silent stroke that let her know how much she meant to him. He nearly smiled at the thought. He loved her deeply, more than life, but at times, reality had a way of edging in sideways.

Chapter Thirty One

THE PARK

Colonial Park

In the dark, the white marble of the band shell stood out like the hulk of a deserted ocean liner.

The last concert had been held three summers ago and the structure now stood abandoned to weeds and weather. The hedges surrounding it had grown thick and wild and the tiled floor of the band shell was criss-crossed with fine cracks. Beneath the stage was a warren of small rooms filled with old lighting equipment, rusted folding chairs, and music stands.

The room containing the stands was the largest and so they had been pushed to one side to accommodate an old mattress, a blanket, a pile of clothing, and a wooden crate filled with cans of food.

Rhino lay on his back peering at the shaft of light filtering through the small hole he had hacked through the wall just below the stage. Through this opening, he had a view of the old dance area and the ornately carved stone benches surrounding it.

He had slept all day as was his habit and felt restless now that night was approaching. But he had to wait a while longer. Too many people were still strolling about.

He rose from the mattress and pulled a cloth over the opening in the wall, then plugged in an extension cord from the next room.

Although the structure had been closed, the electricity, through some oversight, had not been turned off. The dim bulb suited him as he moved about the room. The walls were crumbling cinderblock and concrete and in bad weather, water seeped through the cracks but it had not rained since that time he had surprised the girl on the roof . He moved about the room thinking about it.

"Almost had her. If it wasn't for that sommabitch comin' on the scene. Shoulda minded his own damn business. Stuck to playin' his dumb fuckin' music. Just like his goddamn father. Too damn dumb to do anything but play that dumb-ass music."

He moved about the room aimlessly, then sat down to rummage through the crate. He picked up a can of sardines, looked at it, then threw it back down, deciding that he wasn't hungry, just restless.

He inspected the crate again, trying to figure out what was missing and what he needed to pick up when he went out later.

Prison had taught him how to break into a place, cut the alarm like an expert, and leave without a mark on the door or a dent in the lock.

No forced entry, the police decided. Maybe the proprietor had neglected to lock up properly. Or maybe the clerks themselves had lightened the stock. Fast, easy answers. Quick wrap. Case closed.

He knew better than to hit the same store twice, so he spread his operations wide. South to 110th Street and West to Broadway. He worked in the early hours, just before daybreak, sometimes raiding whole cases of bread and rolls or containers of juice and milk left by the deliverymen. At other times he took only what he was able to stuff in his pockets or under his jacket.

When a patrol car passed, he froze until one night a cop rolled down the window and waved. "Careful in these parts, buddy. You lost?"

And he had shaken head. "No," he said.

The car had driven away and he had stood there, amazed at the revelation, then laughing hard until his face hurt. From a distance, they had mistaken him for a white man. After that, he had learned to walk normally, as if he were headed to the subway for an early morning job.

He stayed clear of the Peacock and the stores on either side of the bar, even after the neon sign had been extinguished for the night and the bird's plume no longer threw its frightening image across the pavement. "Damn lights. They could come on any time. Any time. Just like...."

He squeezed the thought away.

At night, he used the public bathroom in the playground near the swings and once in a while, he wriggled through the fence to swim in the pool – not to bathe but to cool off from the heat of the day. At those times, he stretched naked on the granite bleachers behind the diving board and tried to think of his next move. But his thoughts flew in endless circles and always came back to 1048 and the apartment on the third floor.

Her blinds were always drawn, at least half way, but there had been times when the blinds had been up and the curtains had drifted out of the window to wave like silk scarves. Her voice was like that: fine and silken and floating like light scarves in the breeze. Yet sometimes, when he opened his memory, the sound of her entered his head like a bullet.

He wrestled with memory at those times, and when he invariably lost, he dashed from the stone steps to leap headlong into the pool, but even the shock of the icy water failed to dull the sound of her singing.

*** ***

He peered through the small hole again, gauging the darkness.

"It's okay now but winter be here and the hawk be squawkin' before I know what hit. Shoulda been long gone, dammit. But I gotta try again. This time come up over the other side of the roof from the avenue. And I'll be ready. Not like last time. Don't know what the hell made that noise. Some kind of animal. Maybe they got a dog or somethin' up there. Nearly broke my leg jumpin'. But this time I'm a be ready. I take care of whatever it is, take care of her, and I'm gone." He eased down on the mattress again and pressed his hand to his forehead.

Take care of her.

What did he intend to do. Kill her. Beg her forgiveness. Explain. But what was there to explain.

It was her fault that Tommy got killed in the first place. It was all her fault. None a this wouldna' happened if only she hadda ...

All at once he thought of the fading picture buried in the bottom of Fannie Dillard's bedroom closet – the young girl in the plaid skirt with her hand raised, waving, telling the world-and him- goodbye. He saw the skirt, saw the face that was as familiar to him as his own, but had never heard that voice calling in a soft, silken whisper- bon voyage.

Never said a word. Nuthin'. Just walked away. I never heard her..

He rose and resumed his pacing.

I'm gettin' that picture. It's mine. Nobody else got a right to it.

He wondered what would happen if he showed the picture to Rose. Just burst right in and flash it, up close, so that the faded image of those deep set eyes and curve of mouth in the dark face would say, 'I am you. You are me.'

And then she could understand why all those things had happened the way it did.

And everything would change. She would beg for forgiveness, understanding, and best of all, most of all, she would offer herself to him in a way that would make up for all the bad times he had lived through.

Or. She would glance at the picture and look at him and then at the picture again and open her mouth and the echo of her laughter would dwarf anything he had ever heard.

He fell back, sweating, on the mattress and allowed the pain to curl into his brow.

Chapter Thirty Two

THE VIADUCT

Sara and Theo paused on the viaduct above 155th Street. The sun had moved West toward the ridge of the Palisades and Sugar Hill's façade glistened in the haze. Below the viaduct, the stream of traffic stretched the length of 8th Avenue in a ribbon of light. The Giants were playing and the Polo Grounds was packed, waiting to see Willie Mays hit another one out of the park.

Theo watched the cars for several minutes before he finally spoke."You haven't said a word since we left the movie, Sara. You feeling all right?"

"Yes. I'm fine. Fine."

She rested her arms on the guard rail. A slight breeze, still warm, carried the oiled presence of the Harlem River and Theo wondered aloud if they might stroll across the bridge. They had gone to the RKO Hamilton and decided, when they left the theatre, to walk the long way home –from 146th Street and Broadway to 155th street and then down the viaduct to 7th avenue. It was still early. They were not expected home until 9 o'clock.

"You feel like walking some more?" he asked.

She turned and looked at the bridge. Beyond it, on 161st Street, the grid of floodlights that usually illuminated Yankee Stadium was not on . The team was out of town and against the backdrop of lights from the Polo Grounds, the steel skeleton of the bridge appeared fragile.

"Let's stay here where it's light and bright and things are moving and we don't have to think about what's going to happen."

He gave her a side-long look, and asked, "What? What's going to happen?"

. "Nothing."

"Come on, Sara. It's a mighty peculiar nothing. Something's bothering you and sooner or later- "

He stopped when she held up her hand. "Listen," she whispered. She glanced over her shoulder as stragglers late for the game hurried past. Across the roadway, obscured by the line of traffic, more people moved around an old man walking a small dog.

"Listen," she said again. "Mama and Daddy told me not to tell. They said I shouldn't tell anyone."

She paused and put her hand to her mouth. The sky had faded to hazy twilight and it was difficult to focus on the movement in the street below.

She closed her eyes and sighed. "What's the use. You'll find out anyway and by that time it'll be too late. So what's the use of not telling."

"Not tell what, for God's sake?"

She turned away and looked over the avenue again. Each car had lost its individuality to the night and the stream of head lights shimmered like a jeweled serpent.

"We're going to move," she whispered, staring at the lights "This time we're really leaving. I didn't eavesdrop or overhear them like the last time. They told me directly. To my face. And they're not letting anyone know. I'm not even supposed to tell you. They said a white man came to see Mrs. Dillard. He was looking for someone."

"Who? Who was he looking for?"

"Nobody knows."

"He was probably looking for Rhino."

"But that's just it. Nobody knows and my father's scared to death."

"Why should he be scared? And where are you moving to?"

"I don't know. I don't know."

She put her hand to her head. The questions were coming too fast and the more she talked, the more she realized that she should not have spoken at all. But how could she not say anything.

She put her arms around him and lay her head on his shoulder. Her breath came soft against the side of his neck. "Theo. This can't happen. I won't let it. I will die. I will die."

She remained in his arms, eyes closed, feeling the pulse in his throat as he swallowed. His hands slid from her shoulders to her waist and pressed her to him. They were alone now except for the passing busses that bathed them in the glare of its lighted windows. From the Polo Grounds the hum of anticipation swelled to a low roar. Mays must have stepped to the plate and Theo's voice was lost in the tide of sound.

"What?"

"I said we could leave," he whispered.

"Leave?"

"Yeah. Go away somewhere, maybe Atlantic City and get married."

"Theo-"

"Why not? I could get a job in a band somewhere. Just like my Pop did. I mean, if he did it, then so can I. things aren't that much different from when he was coming up. He used to complain sometimes about how things were, but he and my mom loved each other and they made it work. So could we."

She stepped back but still held to him. She was not able to speak but looked at his eyes, cheekbones, and the full curve of his mouth that she had so eagerly sought in dark of the theatre. She felt again the trembling, the shaking that had earlier overpowered her. Now, still unable to control it, her thoughts spun. What would it take, she wondered, to hold on to this moment, and him, forever.

"Sara, listen." He spoke quickly, trying to push the words out before his courage failed. "Next Saturday, instead of going to the movies again, we'll leave and-"

"Leave? Where will we go? We have no money?"

"I have eighty dollars saved. I was gonna buy a flute. Teach you how to play it."

"Oh, Theo.."

"Well, that can wait. It's you and me now, Sara. I'll have to teach you some other time."

He thought of his mother and the awful pain of her disappointment. In the back of his head, he heard a small voice – her voice- saying, 'don't get fresh with that girl. I trust you. Her mother trusts you. Don't disappoint us'

And he knew that his father, who had said nothing since the 'condom conference- as he had come to call it, had his eye on him also; his father, who didn't miss a trick with one eye closed in a darkroom.

Theo sighed. He wanted his mother's trust and he did try to control himself. Even in the darkness of the theatre when he felt Sara's hand slip from his and come to rest on his thigh. She never looked at him but her touch grew heavy almost immediately after the lights dimmed and he had ached so much that he could not, for the life of him, remember what the movie had been about.

Now control was out and so was trust. They were going to do what they had to do. He remembered what his father had said about Thurgood Marshall. It took struggle to realize a dream. He had planned to make the dream come true, not only to see the smile on his mother and father at graduation but to please himself also. He would be a famous attorney and play jazz for relaxation. He and Sara would live in a big house on Strivers row- with a special music room that held all the instruments he could imagine. He and Sara were going to travel and do the things they read about in Ebony magazine.

But Rhino had come out of nowhere, like an old haunt, tearing through their dreams.

He gazed at Sara, trying to look beyond the excitement in her eyes and gauge the fear.

"My father will come after us," she said.

"So will mine. Are you scared?"

She shook her head. "A little. No. A lot. A lot."

The roar in the Polo Grounds erupted and was so intense that the concrete pavement of the viaduct seemed to shake. The crowd began a chant "Say Hey! Say Hey! Willie Mays!!"

Theo said something but Sara put her fingers to her lips and pointed to the end of the walkway.

7th Avenue was quieter. They walked past the Flash Inn and glanced at the crowd at the bar watching the game on television. Glasses were lifted in toasts and some drinkers were also shouting but not as loudly. Sara ignored this and tried to make sense of what Theo had said.

He wanted her to go away with him. But they weren't going away. They were running away.

She was turning a corner in her life. A door was closing that she could never go back to open. How had this happened? Right now, she needed time to think, needed to walk one more time, possibly her last, through 139th street - Strivers Row –to fix in her mind's eye the homes with the iron filigree balconies and windows with delicate curtains draped in a fashion that seemed to safeguard and keep precious the lives inside. A life she would never experience if she went away.

And she wanted to remember the leafy canopy of linden trees lining the curbs and the brass plaques in front of some of the houses that indicated an M.D. resided there. If she left now, her name would never appear on one.

She stopped under a street lamp. A light film of perspiration covered the bridge of her nose and her eyes shone as if she were suddenly feverish.

"My father won't come after us, Theo. He won't have the strength. He works so hard. He's tired. His job, his life, all his worries have… made him so old.

"Sometimes, at night when he comes in, I watch him and my eyelids itch from holding back my tears. If I leave and throw away my scholarship, it will be the end of him. It will kill him."

Her words seemed to rest on the air and she was surprised at how much like her mother she sounded. "This will kill him," she said again.

Theo touched her face, his fingers brushing the lobe of her ear. "I know. I know. But it was- a thought, Sara. Something that would keep us together, somehow. But I'll think of something. I'm not giving up, you hear. We can't give up."

They resumed their walk in silence and 7th Avenue seemed more crowded now that night had fallen. Everyone was dressed up. A caravan of Buicks, Cadillacs, and Oldsmobiles – pulled up to the curb at 137th Street and several couples stepped out in tuxedos and gowns and strolled into the Renaissance Ballroom carrying party platters and cases of champagne. The women wore their beauty like a gift and the men moved in the manner of peacocks, proud, surefooted. Their laughter flowed like a current and Theo wanted to cup his hand and capture the sound of such stunning assurance. Wrap his fingers around it to hold like a shield against what was to come.

Theo had earlier planned to take Sara for a soda at Snookie's Sugar Bowl, the snack shop that catered largely to the college crowd. Theo sometimes hung out there, although college for him was still a year away. But he looked at the varsity letters and he noticed the way the girls smiled at the guys in those sweaters.

The place was always crowded with talk of fraternities and plans for the future and he couldn't wait to become part of that.

Now they passed the shop without stopping and he stared straight ahead, wondering why he hadn't killed Rhino when he had the chance. He'd been angry enough to do it. Why didn't he? Then all this would never have come up.

He glanced at Sara. She was quiet and he knew she was thinking her own thoughts so he did not disturb her. They walked slowly, tracing their way up 7th Avenue, each footfall bringing them closer to the dissolution of their dreams.

At the corner, she pulled at his arm and stared down the block.

"No," she murmured.

Theo looked at her. She was staring without seeing.

"No .No." her voice was barely audible and he had to lean close. He followed her gaze but could see nothing.

She let go of his arm and stepped away. Her eyes were too bright and Theo felt a small shiver go through him. Before he could speak, she whispered, "we're moving as soon possible, probably two in weeks. Oh, we can't. We can't – I can't leave you. I can't leave you."

She turned away and walked quickly down the block. He had to hurry to catch up.

Chapter Thirty Three
APT2A

"How come you can't do something?"

"Because I can't, Theo. Didn't you just say that no one was supposed to know? Didn't you just say that?"

"Yeah, Dad, but – "

"So what am I supposed to do? If they move, it doesn't mean that you can't see the girl any more. When things quiet down, you might be able to – "

"By then, it'll be too late, Dad. You don't understand. By then, she'll be gone."

"Theo. Take it easy. And sit down, boy. You making me nervous."

Matthew lit another cigarette and watched his son pace the living room floor. Theo's striped shirt was open at the neck and his hands were jammed deep in his khaki slacks. A light sheen covered his forehead and his breathing sounded as if he had been running, running to grasp a prize that seemed just a finger's length away.

Matthew averted his gaze and exhaled. The acrid residue was hot on his tongue and he tamped the cigarette out.

Damn. Every time I make up my mind to give up these cigs, something pops up to change my mind. This boy thinks he's the only one on the planet ever had a hard time with a woman. He ain't seen nuthin' yet. I got stories that would make his hair curl. But Sandy's in the kitchen and she don't need to hear none of that. Later, I'll tell him all about it later.

... There were the tough guys, hard guys, good guys, all brought low by love. I remember guys on the road killing themselves in one night gigs only

to come home and find some other shoes under their bed. Or the guy who unlocked his door and his pad was cleaned out so good, even the roaches had left. And more than one cat stuck his key in the door to find it didn't fit anymore. I remember one who came home and just went nuts. Chick smiling, telling him a bundle was on the way and when it arrived, it looked more like the cat's ace buddy than like him.

Shoot!! This boy think he got trouble. His stuff is fluff.

But when he glanced at Theo who had not stopped pacing, his attitude softened.

"Okay. I see you trying to wear a hole in this rug, so look here. What I can do is try to, you know, approach her dad, kind of casually, and see if he mentions anything. I won't bring up this conversation. If he brings it up, then I'll try to find out where they're headed, okay? That's all I can do."

Theo looked stricken and Matthew could not find the words to comfort him, except to say, "I't's gonna be all right, son. It's gonna be all right."

Theo said nothing but picked up his horn and turned to leave.

"Wait a minute. Where're you going?"

"Sorry, Dad. I forgot."

Matthew looked at him and knew he had been headed for the roof to try to soften the hard knot forming in his chest; to the roof where no one, not even the poker players, went anymore. Word of the midnight creeper had spread and now sunset was the signal to close all windows. At night, everyone slept locked in the small ovens of their bedrooms.

Theo placed the horn in its case and moved to the window. His gait was unsteady and Matthew thought of a small craft that had slipped its mooring, wheeling in turbulence, about to drift out to sea.

"Listen, I got another idea," Matthew said.

"What?" Theo, his voice a disinterested whisper, did not turn around. "What?" he said again.

"The guys will be doing something for Rose next week end. We're getting her ready to get back in the groove. We'll get Stan to drop in on the party. You know, all this time, he's never stepped into the Alley. If he pops in, he might relax. We'll talk. Maybe we can persuade him to change his plans."

"You think so? Sara said his mind was pretty much made up."

"We'll see. Who knows? And since we're backing Rose, how about if you sit in?"

"What??" Theo turned from the window to face his father.

"Just for a hot five," Matthew said, holding up his hand. "A hot five, not the whole night."

"Dad, you mean it? Me? Sit in?"

"I think you can handle it."

Matthew saw the excitement in Theo's eyes and shook his head.

A minute ago, this boy was ready to fall in a coma 'cause life wasn't goin' right. He was about to croak from a coronary and now he's ready to jam. Damn. If love ain't a switch, I don't know what is.

Ah, anything in particular you want to play? You'll be doin' a solo, you know."

Theo put his hand to his chest and Matthew wondered if indeed the boy had chest pain.

"A solo? Dad, I can't do a- "

"Yes, you can."

"But I –"

"Yes, you can," Matthew said, rising from the chair. "You can do anything you put your mind to. Go inside your head, find the sound, and listen. It's there. It was always there. I heard it enough times when you sat at that window."

Theo removed the horn from the case again and angled it before him, examining it like a newly received gift. "Okay. I know what you mean."

"So what'll you be playing? I gotta let the guys know tonight."

Theo went to the window and looked out. The courtyard was quiet except for a thread of blues drifting from a small radio somewhere. He was silent and Matthew wondered if he was communing with his muse upstairs. A few minutes passed before he said, "what a difference a day makes. I like that. That's what I'll play."

"Sounds good to me," Matthew said.

Theo went to his room. A minute later, sound flowed from behind the closed door. Matthew strolled to the window and opened it wider to allow the evening air to blow in. People on the avenue, were going about business as usual. A woman with a child in her arms waited at the bus stop. An old man with a cane lounged against the lamp post waiting for the light to change and cars to glide to a stop. A young couple, arms locked, strolled by, oblivious of everything but each other.

And Matthew wondered about them. Was the old man aching from age or injury? Was he reconciled to the fact that the cane had become a part of him? What struggles did the woman with the child have to deal with, and where had she found the strength? And the lovers, had they yet dealt with a pain so special, no one else was able to understand?

Theo's riff pulled him from his reverie. He left the window and went to the dresser to pull a shirt from the drawer and a tie from the closet. Then he glanced in the mirror and took a deep breath. Theo was still playing "what a difference a day makes."

What a difference indeed. He listened and whistled softly as he dressed.

Chapter Thirty Four

4 A.M.

"So Rose is ready for the spotlight?" Blue asked, pausing at the last table. The crowd had gone and only Matthew and Cyrus remained. The jukebox was turned low and the sound of Johnny Moore and the Three Blazers whispered through the empty room.

Matthew sat at the piano and Cyrus leaned against the bar in the dim light.

"Rose is ready, "Cyrus said, "and she's starting again right here. She always said she wanted to sing here first. Test her pipes."

"You know we haven't heard a note since Tommy got killed," Blue said.

"But she's still taking lessons," Matthew said, running his fingers down the keys. "Miss Adele is her teacher so you know she can't lose."

Blue shrugged and swept the mounds of plastic cups into a carton. Then he emptied the ashtrays and cleaned the tables with a wet cloth. "I know she and Tommy was real tight," he said, "but damn, two years is a long time to burn the candle. I mean, it's not like he's coming back."

"Maybe not," Matthew said, "but all I can say is I haven't seen her with another man since it happened. I mean Tommy must've been a heavy hitter. Kept Babe and Rose smilin' so if you ain't heard a note, don't that tell you something?"

"Yeah. It tells me that Babe collected the insurance and Rose is still in that damn factory."

"Not for long," Cyrus interjeted. "She's ready to change lanes. With Matt and the guys backing her, I know she can do it."

"One more thing," Matthew said, rising from the piano. "Theo is doing a solo for the gig."

Blue stopped and stared at Matthew in the dim light. "Matt, the kid's under age. We servin' heavy brew in here. How're we gonna pull that?"

"Think of something, Blue. Maybe like a birthday. Send a special invite to everybody in the house. And put a sign outside just for the night. That should work."

"It better or my payout gets doubled."

"Look, man," Matthew said, moving to the bar to pick up his unfinished drink. "I got a problem with the boy. Sara and her folks are moving. He got the word and now he's strolling like a blind man. He's bumping into furniture."

"Damn, I can't remember ever being in that condition."

"It's love, Blue. And how you gonna remember something you ain't never had."

"Now that's cold, my friend. That's ice."

"Just kidding. But the boy's in a trance. Usually when he has something on his mind, he'd go up on the roof and blow some notes and he'd come back in the house, feeling better."

"Man, I know you're not telling him to hit the roof, not with Rhino maybe doing the midnight creep."

"We don't even know if it is Rhino. Could be anybody. So Tar Beach is closed for the duration. There's no life guard on duty. That's why I want him down here next week end. Matter of fact, I already mentioned it and he's looking forward to it."

"And speaking of which, I got a call earlier this week," Blue said. "My 3-2 man had some stuff about our friend. Seems all those souvenirs, those bruises and bumps Rhino came home with was compliments of Babe."

Matthew and Cyrus had taken a seat at one of the tables. The music stopped and a small silence now surrounded them. Matthew glanced at Blue and shrugged in disbelief.

"Babe got inside the walls? I knew she pulled a little weight but how'd she manage that?"

"Dollars makes everything do-able," Blue said, popping a beer and joining them at the table. "Somehow she got word in along with some heavy cash. And special instructions. Wanted Rhino taken care of, not killed but beat so steady and so bad, he'd know he wasn't in there for no short time vacation. The guards split the stash and was happy to split his head.

"She paid for six months of treatment and it was one hour every night after the lights went out. They used their flashlights. In the dark, with the beams in his face, he couldn't see so nobody could say who did what.

"Even after the dollars stopped, the guards didn't.

It was like dessert after a meal and they had taken a liking to it. One time it had got so heavy, he stopped breathing. They popped him into the infirmary claiming there had been some beef. Nobody could find the other inmate. Things was getting out of control and the warden couldn't stand no spotlight. He pulled a string, broke bread with a commissioner and Rhino got cut loose. Supposed to do a ten bid but walked in two."

"And so he comes back meaner than when he left," Cyrus murmured, putting his glass down. "A fine example of the law of unintended consequences."

"So," Blue said, rising from the table. "He got what he deserved and now he slides back here to turn the whole damn place upside down. Folks are planning to move, cards cancelled because people scared to be on the roof. Fire escapes blocked. Windows locked. Everybody lookin' over their shoulder. Shit. A damn plague couldn't have done this much damage. If I had known what the deal was, I would've thrown in some extra change and got the job done right."

Chapter Thirty Five

APT 3A

Cyrus let himself in to the apartment and found Effie in the bedroom sitting at the small dressing table.

"You look good," he whispered, bending to kiss her. She caught his gaze in the mirror and put the hairbrush down.

"What do you think?" she said, turning to face him.

"I think it looks fine. Your hair looks beautiful."

"You think everyone will like it?"

"I think folks tend to mind other people's business too much, and they don't have time to tend to their own."

"Oh, Cyrus, that's..that's not what I asked you."

"I know, Baby. Are we going to argue about it?"

"No, but I-"

"I know how you feel," he said, pulling a chair up to sit beside her. "You haven't taken the scarf off since you changed your style, so it's time. And it's bound to be a surprise. It's been two weeks. I think you should surprise the hell out of everyone. Walk into that party on my arm tomorrow and surprise the hell out of everybody. Let 'em see what a beauty you are."

"Cyrus. Cyrus. You know how nervous – "

"Naturally you'll be nervous but Sandra and Theo will be there. And Matthew even persuaded Clothilde and Stan to show up."

"He did?"

"Yep. It's sort of a farewell party. They're planning to move, you know."

"I know, and I'm going to miss them. Sara spent so many hours on the roof with me. It won't be the same anymore."

She turned to the mirror again and picked up the brush. Cyrus leaned back, watching as she studied her face for imperfections that were not there. The dark hair brought out red highlights in her brown skin and the thin curve of her brows were accentuated in the soft light. Her eyes were large dark ovals but he knew from her movements that her husband had never told her these things, had never told her that she was beautiful and deserved to know this.

She deserves to be told a lot of things, but one thing at a time. I can't mention that Rose will be singing. I do that and Effie will find some reason not to come. This has got to stop. Sooner or later, they'll –

"This dress is gorgeous," Effie said opening the large box and pulling away the tissue paper. She was on her feet, holding the garment against her. Then she leaned over. "Cyrus," she whispered," you are so good to me, good for me, and just plain good. Period. God knows, I love you so much."

He closed his eyes and drew in the scent of her crème sachet when she kissed him.. The dress slid to the floor as he reached up to ease her onto his lap.

"Wait, Cyrus. The dress. Wait."

"Baby, there's more where that came from. Don't worry about it..."

His mouth found the hollow near the nape of her neck. "Aah, Effie, don't worry about it, Baby."

"Cyrus – "

"Hmmm. These brassieres should be made with no straps, Baby."

"Cyrus – "

" – And...and no hooks."

He eased the brassiere away and cupped her breasts in his hands. "Girl, look at you. You don't know how beautiful you are..."

"Oh!"

Her fingers reached for the small lamp on the table but he pulled her hand back. "Unh, unh. Leave the light. I want to see your face when you – "

"I usually close my eyes when I open my mouth.." she whispered.

"Well, I want to see it," he said, easing her to the floor to lay beside him. His fingers slid between her breasts and minutes later, traced a light line to her hips. " I want to see your face, Baby."

Chapter Thirty Six

9P.M.

The darkness was impenetrable and Effie regretted leaving the flashlight on the kitchen table. She had picked it up but Cyrus had laughed. "Baby, that takes all the mystery out of it. Darkness is part of the package," he had smiled and she had nodded and left it on the table.

She managed to navigate the creaking stairs into the courtyard but entering the corridor was like walking into a wall. The musicians had not yet arrived and there was no sound to guide her.

She clung to Cyrus as they walked. "Why doesn't Blue put in some lights?" she whispered. "Somebody could fall dead in here and not be found for a year."

They moved in slow, measured steps and she felt the crunch of gravel under her high heels and thin soles. Then she stopped abruptly, nearly tripping him.

"Are there any rats down here?"

"Come on, Effie. It wouldn't be Harlem without the rats, but they know this is a special occasion. We made a deal and they left town. Just for tonight."

He laughed but she did not join him. She knew it was a party, a special farewell for Stan and Clothilde. She had not wanted them to leave, but Cyrus said that they'd already made up their minds and that was that. She wondered how Theo was going to manage. And poor Sara. How was she going to take it?

She shook her head and moved closer to Cyrus. In the dark, his step was sure and steady but he held her hand in a grip that made her wonder if he was afraid she might change her mind and retreat back to her apartment, perhaps to get the scarf that she had hidden under for so long.

The darkness pressed against her like a living thing and she expected something to float out of nowhere and brush her face with web-like fingers.

The door to the club was a few feet away. She strained to hear a note, a voice, but even the jukebox had not yet been turned on and all she heard was the sound of her own heartbeat. It seemed loud and she wondered if Cyrus heard it. She tried to find his face, to see, but could only make out the outline of his strong jaw. Everything else was lost in the void.

"They're probably still setting up," he whispered. "They ordered a lot of food, you know, plus balloons and other stuff. Blue's probably still getting everything ready. Maybe I should've come down earlier to give him a hand."

They approached the door and his grip seemed to tighten but she did not mind. Better, she thought, for the hand to hurt than to make a wrong move and stumble into something she could not find her way out of.

Chapter Thirty Seven
THE PARK

Leaving Colonial Park

Nearly nine p.m. and noise from the playground still drifted toward him.

Rhino lifted the cloth covering the hole and scanned the area. No one was within his angle of vision but he decided to wait a few more minutes. He turned to survey the room one last time.

All I need is this bag. Small enough. Leave this other junk. I travel light, I travel fast

He lifted the flap again. The playground noise had ebbed, replaced now by the thick, frenetic whine of cicadas on the night air. He picked up the small bag, creaked open the rusted door, and stepped outside. His shirt stuck to his skin in the humid air. He smelled his perspiration and ignored it and walked faster. A block away, he turned into 147th street and quickly entered the corner building.

Walk along the roof, duck them lights, all them lights from that fuckin' bird. They far enough. Can't touch me. The wall onto 1048 is high but I climbed it enough times. Get up that roof, then take the stairs. I still got my key and I know she ain't had sense enough to change that lock. Thinks I'm gone and she don't have to think about it no more.

Get that picture. Rose need to know everything could've been a whole lot different if only she'd –

He climbed over the hedge–like barrier of the building fronting 8th Avenue and came to the adjoining wall of 1048. He stepped back, took a running leap and hoisted himself up, scaling the nine foot height as easily a cat. On the roof, he opened the door to the stairway and listened. It was too quiet. He decided against stepping inside and moved to the fire escape instead.

Two flights down, Fannie Dillard's window was open. He peered in, listening for movement. A second later, he was standing in her bedroom.

Her bed was undisturbed, covered with the familiar pink starched linen bedspread. A pyramid of porcelain faced dolls was stacked against the pillow and their glass eyes seemed to follow him.

In the dim light, the ceiling fan, immobile, cast a spidery image against the wall.

Gotta git the fuck outta here. Where the hell is she this time of night? Who the hell cares. I'm in. Git what I came for and anything else layin' loose. Then git the hell on out.

The photograph was still under the quilts – wrapped in plastic just as he'd left it and he had no time to wonder if Fannie Dillard had looked at it and put it back rather than placing it in a frame. He didn't care. On the dresser, there was cash, a small gold watch, and two pearl necklaces and that–along with the picture- was stuffed into his bag. He tiptoed through the living room and into the kitchen. The cat clock read 9:15. He took a can of beer from the fridge, slipped it into his bag and made his way to the hall. He stepped outside and smiled as he locked the door behind him.

Maybe she went to the store. She gonna be surprised when she git back. Now for the other surprise.

Rose. He remained on the stairs between the landing, listening, but there was no sound and no movement. The place was quiet for a Friday night.

Maybe somebody died. Maybe they all at a funeral or something. Hell with it. Knock on her door. She gotta be home. If–

He made his way back to the roof landing.

A minute later, a door opened on the floor below and he wondered if it was who he thought it was. The footsteps were light and fast and heading up the steps. He shrank back, wondering what to do.

Then several floors below that, he heard someone else. Footsteps that were lighter, slower, coming up the stairs.

Shit! Too much traffic. Fuck it. Take a chance.

He hugged the bag to him and remained still, listening to the sounds approaching him. Then he breathed in a familiar fragrance that almost made his heart stop.

It's her! I know it. I know it. She's coming up here. She's coming here to me. To me.

The other, fainter, sounds two floors below had stopped and so he concentrated on the near sound, the light, fast, click of heels rounding the bend, moving toward him.

He waited in the dark, as still as stone.

Rose was coming up to the roof.

Chapter 38

9:15P.M.

In the hall, Rose leaned against the banister.

..No music yet. Everyone's probably waiting for me to show. Well, Tommy, this is it and you're not here to see it happen. If things had been different, you'd be in the front row, at that table where you sat that night. But I know you're near. I can feel it.

And you know Blue and everyone is looking out for me also.

She touched the diamond earrings and the velvet purse he had given her.

Everyone's downstairs already, but this'll only take

A second to get myself together and say a prayer. And say thanks to you because things are turning just as you said.

She moved up the stairs, not all the way just far enough to glimpse the night sky through the door opened to the roof. A sliver of moon hung beneath a blanket of stars.

She stopped, wanting to close her eyes to the prayer but the landing smelled as if someone had left a bag of garbage there.

Chapter Thirty Nine

9:15PM

Two floors below, Effie sat on the steps wondering if she had done the right thing.

...told him to go help Blue. And not worry about me. I was only going to the ladies room. I would be right back. Anyway, that's what I had intended.

But once she had made her way around the tables that were beginning to fill up, and had taken refuge in the small room, she had gazed in the oval mirror over the basin, stared at the ashen skin under the strange hair and then closed her eyes.

...why did he do this? Rose is coming here. She's singing tonight and he didn't tell me. Didn't say a word. I had to see those signs on the tables and see her face staring from that poster over the bar.

She leaned over the basin and studied her own face.

This wasn't what I had planned... not at all. Not at all.

She thought of her scarf and frowned, wishing she had put one in her purse. But the purse was too small. And Cyrus would probably have said she didn't need it. Just as she had not needed the flashlight.

"Damn.."

She looked around, wondering what to do, then opened the wall cabinet. It was empty except for a few bars of soap. She had no idea what she was looking for and why she was doing it. She inspected the shelf under the basin that held cleaning equipment; more soap and a small pail.

And someone, perhaps the electrician, the plumber, or maybe Blue, had left a flashlight wrapped in a small square of heavy tarp.

She unwrapped it and walked back into the main room where Cyrus was behind the bar helping Blue stock the shelves. His back was turned. The room was getting crowded and Matthew had come in and was setting up the bandstand.

And Theo is with him.

She watched the boy open his case and remove his clarinet.

He's going to play tonight. Seems like the surprises just keep on coming.

She remained near the door and when it opened again, she eased out through the flow of newcomers.

I'll be back before he even knows I'm gone.

Navigating the corridor was faster with the light in her hand. It also helped that several persons were in the courtyard, nodding in surprise as they passed her. She smiled. Perhaps she did not need the scarf after all.

In the lobby, she moved lightly up the steps. She had not worn high heels in ages and her toes were cramped and the straps cut into her ankles.

First thing I'll do is change these damn killer shoes. Take them off right now. The music's started already. Maybe I can manage. Hell, no, even if Cyrus gives me that hot oil treatment. Well, maybe. Ah, maybe, he'll even-

She sat on the steps, undecided, with the shoes in her hand, when she heard the scream.

Chapter Forty

MEETING

His arm had snaked out and around her neck, choking off sound.

"Listen, Rose, and listen to me good," he whispered. "You yell again and it'll be the last sound you ever make."

His hand dropped to her waist and he dragged her out to the roof toward the circle of chairs.

"I..I got something to show you." His words slid out, hissing. "Something that'll make you.."

He pushed her to down into a chair and stood over her. "Something that'll change your mind about everything."

She stared up at him, open mouthed, shaking, and it was several seconds before she found her voice.

"What?? What are you doing? Nothing you got will ever make a difference. Tommy's dead and you did it. You did it! I hate you. I wish you were dead too, you horrible, ugly –"

Her words were cut off when his fist hit her face. "I told you to shut up, bitch, and that's what I meant. Nothing'll make a difference? That's what you think. Looka here. Is that what you said when you cut out on me??"

"What??"

"That's right. You ran. Cut out. Disappeared. And here's the proof. You can't fool me!"

He shoved the picture in her face but she shrank from it, did not look at it. Instead, she stared at him. In the dim light, the planes and angles of his face seemed coated with chalk. His eyes were large holes behind the lens of his glasses.

"You are crazy, Rhino. Always was. Always will be. You're crazy. I never did anything to you. You went and killed Tommy and you got away with it. I hate you. If I had gun right now I'd kill you the way you killed him. I wish you was dead."

"Wish I was dead? We gonna see about that. I'm a make you change your mind if I have to- "

He bent toward her and she spun away from him and off the chair, crawling out of the circle on her hands and knees. "Don't you touch me! I'd die first than let you – "

She got to her feet but he grabbed her as she tried to run. "You whore! Still runnin' but this time you ain't goin' nowhere but with me! You goin' with me. I'm a kill you anyway 'cause all this is your fault. Leavin' me with no name, no home, no nuthin'!!"

"What the hell are you talkin' about?"

"You know what I'm talkin' about."

"You are crazy."

"Go ahead," he whispered. "Scream. See if they hear you. Music's on now. Loud. Nobody'll hear nuthin'."

He snatched at her purse. The clasp opened and Tommy's razor fell to the ground between them. He scooped it up before she could grab it.

"You bitch! You was gonna use this on me, wasn't you? The same way Tommy used one on me.

Remember? Well, I'll show you right now."

He swung the blade in a wide arc and Rose, screaming, ducked under it.

"Help!! Somebody help me!"

She tried to run again and he grabbed her and held the knife to her throat. She could feel the cold steel under her chin.

"Yes, this is way you goin'. I'll slice you the way he sliced me. And I'll throw you over the side and nobody'll know nuthin 'till tomorrow. How you like that. Fix you so you don't run anymore. You won't be runnin' no more. Slice you the way he-"

When the arc of light flashed, he dropped his arm. He spun around and Rose scrambled out of his reach. She ran from the circle. He chased her but stopped short when the light hit him again in the face.

Effie held the flashlight waist high, sweeping the area. "Sara! Sara! What's going on, girl?"

:"No! No! Effie! It's me! It's Rose. Help me. Help me."

"What?? What's going on up here?"

Effie arced the light and Rhino froze, then dropped the razor and edged away, scrambling back from Rose and the light. Several feet away, he tripped and nearly fell. He slowed, then moved again, bewildered. The light caught him again and he recoiled.

"Get the fuck-"

Rose ran toward Effie and collapsed. "Effie, help me. Please. Please. Help me. Don't let him do this. Don't let him."

"What happened??" Effie juggled the flashlight and pressed the high beam, sweeping the area.

Rhino turned to run and Effie had no time to think about why she was chasing him. She was running and did not feel the soft tar beneath her bare feet. Did not think about her dress or the scarf or the picture that had smiled down at her from the poster over the bar. All of that had been washed away in Rose's plaintive sound. Rose was crying now and struggling to run beside her. Her left eye was swollen, nearly shut. "We gotta stop him, Effie. We gotta..."

He had jumped down to the adjoining roof nine feet below. He dodged out of the way as the beam of light followed, tracking him along the perimeter high above the avenue.

"There he is! There he is!!!

Rose hysterical, was shouting, and leaning near the edge. "He's running! He's running. He's getting away."

Her screams carried down to the courtyard but was lost in the noise of the music.

"Wait! There he goes!"

The beam turned into a searchlight and caught him in its arc. He stopped, spread his arms wide, and cried out, "See, Ma! This time I'm the one that's leavin'. Me! I'm leavin' you. Now see how you like it. See how you like it, Ma!!"

He glanced up as if searching the night sky, held his arms out, and stumbled blindly toward the edge.

Epilogue

Fannie Dillard moved to Philadelphia a week after the funeral, which Blue paid for. His man at the three two was true to his word and so the inquiry was brief.

Two weeks later, Rose closed the set in the Blind Alley before a standing room only crowd.

Effie, Cyrus, Stan and Clothilde shared a table up front and led the applause which lasted for ten minutes. Effie joined in also, and the ring which

Cyrus had placed on her finger moments before, sparked in the light.

CPSIA information can be obtained at www.ICGtesting.com
Printed in the USA
BVOW030720210312

285701BV00005B/189/P